# PROMETHEUS UNBOUND

## A LYRICAL DRAMA IN FOUR ACTS

PERCY BYSSHE SHELLEY

Black Box Press
Los Angeles

NOTE: *Prometheus Bound* is in the public domain and may be performed without paying royalties.

ISBN 978-0-6151-4975-2

First Black Box Press Edition

# PREFACE

The Greek tragic writers, in selecting as their subject any portion of their national history or mythology, employed in their treatment of it a certain arbitrary discretion. They by no means conceived themselves bound to adhere to the common interpretation or to imitate in story as in title their rivals and predecessors. Such a system would have amounted to a resignation of those claims to preference over their competitors which incited the composition. The Agamemnonian story was exhibited on the Athenian theatre with as many variations as dramas.

I have presumed to employ a similar license. The *Prometheus Unbound* of Aeschylus supposed the reconciliation of Jupiter with his victim as the price of the disclosure of the danger threatened to his empire by the consummation of his marriage with Thetis. Thetis, according to this view of the subject, was given in marriage to Peleus, and Prometheus, by the permission of Jupiter, delivered from his captivity by Hercules. Had I framed my story on this model, I should have done no more than have attempted to restore the lost drama of Aeschylus; an ambition which, if my preference to this mode of treating the subject had incited me to cherish, the recollection of the high comparison such an attempt would challenge might well abate. But, in truth, I was averse from a catastrophe so feeble as that of reconciling the Champion with the Oppressor of mankind. The moral interest of the fable, which is so powerfully sustained by the sufferings and endurance of Prometheus, would be annihilated if we could conceive of him as unsaying his high language and quailing before his successful and perfidious adversary. The only imaginary being resembling in any degree Prometheus, is Satan; and Prometheus is, in my judgement, a more poetical character than Satan, because, in addition to courage, and majesty, and firm and patient opposition to omnipotent force, he is susceptible of being described as exempt from the taints of ambition, envy, revenge, and a desire for personal aggrandisement, which, in the Hero of *Paradise Lost*, interfere with the interest. The character of Satan engenders in the mind a pernicious casuistry which leads us to weigh his faults with his wrongs, and to excuse the former because the latter exceed all measure. In the minds of those who consider that magnificent fiction with a religious feeling it engenders something worse. But Prometheus is, as it were, the type of the highest

3

perfection of moral and intellectual nature, impelled by the purest and the truest motives to the best and noblest ends.

This Poem was chiefly written upon the mountainous ruins of the Baths of Caracalla, among the flowery glades, and thickets of odoriferous blossoming trees, which are extended in ever winding labyrinths upon its immense platforms and dizzy arches suspended in the air. The bright blue sky of Rome, and the effect of the vigorous awakening spring in that divinest climate, and the new life with which it drenches the spirits even to intoxication, were the inspiration of this drama.

The imagery which I have employed will be found, in many instances, to have been drawn from the operations of the human mind, or from those external actions by which they are expressed. This is unusual in modern poetry, although Dante and Shakespeare are full of instances of the same kind: Dante indeed more than any other poet, and with greater success. But the Greek poets, as writers to whom no resource of awakening the sympathy of their contemporaries was unknown, were in the habitual use of this power; and it is the study of their works (since a higher merit would probably be denied me) to which I am willing that my readers should impute this singularity.

One word is due in candour to the degree in which the study of contemporary writings may have tinged my composition, for such has been a topic of censure with regard to poems far more popular, and indeed more deservedly popular, than mine. It is impossible that any one who inhabits the same age with such writers as those who stand in the foremost ranks of our own, can conscientiously assure himself that his language and tone of thought may not have been modified by the study of the productions of those extraordinary intellects. It is true, that, not the spirit of their genius, but the forms in which it has manifested itself, are due less to the peculiarities of their own minds than to the peculiarity of the moral and intellectual condition of the minds among which they have been produced. Thus a number of writers possess the form, whilst they want the spirit of those whom, it is alleged, they imitate; because the former is the endowment of the age in which they live, and the latter must be the uncommunicated lightning of their own mind.

The peculiar style of intense and comprehensive imagery which distinguishes the modern literature of England has not been, as a general power, the product of the imitation of any particular writer. The mass of capabilities remains at every period materially the same; the circumstances which awaken it to action perpetually change. If England were divided into forty republics, each equal in population and extent to Athens, there is no reason to suppose but that, under institutions not more perfect than those of Athens, each would produce philosophers and poets equal to those who (if we except Shakespeare) have never been surpassed. We owe the great writers of the golden age of our literature to that fervid awakening of the public mind which shook to dust the oldest and most oppressive form of the Christian religion. We owe Milton to the progress and development of the same spirit: the sacred Milton was, let it ever be remembered, a republican, and a bold inquirer into morals and religion. The great writers of our own age are, we have reason to suppose, the companions and forerunners of some unimagined change in our social condition or the opinions which cement it. The cloud of mind is discharging its collected lightning, and the equilibrium between institutions and opinions is now restoring, or is about to be restored.

As to imitation, poetry is a mimetic art. It creates, but it creates by combination and representation. Poetical abstractions are beautiful and new, not because the portions of which they are composed had no previous existence in the mind of man or in nature, but because the whole produced by their combination has some intelligible and beautiful analogy with those sources of emotion and thought, and with the contemporary condition of them: one great poet is a masterpiece of nature which another not only ought to study but must study. He might as wisely and as easily determine that his mind should no longer be the mirror of all that is lovely in the visible universe as exclude from his contemplation the beautiful which exists in the writings of a great contemporary. The pretence of doing it would be a presumption in any but the greatest; the effect, even in him, would be strained, unnatural and ineffectual. A poet is the combined product of such internal powers as modify the nature of others; and of such external influences as excite and sustain these powers; he is not one, but both. Every man's mind is, in this respect, modified by all the objects of nature and art; by every word and every suggestion which he ever admitted to act upon his consciousness; it is the mirror upon which all forms are reflected, and in which they compose one form. Poets, not otherwise than philosophers, painters, sculptors and musicians, are, in one sense, the creators, and, in another, the creations, of their age. From this subjection the loftiest do not escape. There is a similarity between Homer and Hesiod, between Aeschylus and Euripides, between Virgil and Horace, between Dante and Petrarch, between Shakespeare and Fletcher, between Dryden and Pope; each has a generic resemblance under which their specific distinctions are arranged. If this similarity be the result of imitation, I am willing to confess that I have imitated.

Let this opportunity be conceded to me of acknowledging that I have, what a Scotch philosopher characteristically terms, 'a passion for reforming the world'—what passion incited him to write and publish his book, he omits to explain. For my part I had rather be damned with Plato and Lord Bacon, than go to Heaven with Paley and Malthus. But it is a mistake to suppose that I dedicate my poetical compositions solely to the direct enforcement of reform, or that I consider them in any degree as containing a reasoned system on the theory of human life. Didactic poetry is my abhorrence; nothing can be equally well expressed in prose that is not tedious and supererogatory in verse. My purpose has hitherto been simply to familiarise the highly refined imagination of the more select classes of poetical readers with beautiful idealisms of moral excellence; aware that until the mind can love, and admire, and trust, and hope, and endure, reasoned principles of moral conduct are seeds cast upon the highway of life which the unconscious passenger tramples into dust, although they would bear the harvest of his happiness. Should I live to accomplish what I purpose, that is, produce a systematical history of what appear to me to be the genuine elements of human society, let not the advocates of injustice and superstition flatter themselves that I should take Aeschylus rather than Plato as my model.

The having spoken of myself with unaffected freedom will need little apology with the candid; and let the uncandid consider that they injure me less than their own hearts and minds by misrepresentation. Whatever talents a person may possess to amuse and instruct others, be they ever so inconsiderable, he is yet bound to exert them: if his attempt be ineffectual, let the punishment of an unaccomplished purpose have been sufficient; let none trouble themselves to heap the dust of oblivion upon his efforts; the pile they raise will betray his grave which might otherwise have been unknown.

—PERCY BYSSHE SHELLEY

# DRAMATIS PERSONÆ.

PROMETHEUS.
DEMOGORGON.
JUPITER.
THE EARTH.
OCEAN.
APOLLO.
MERCURY.
OCEANIDES: ASIA, PANTHEA, IONE.
HERCULES.
THE PHANTASM OF JUPITER.
THE SPIRIT OF THE EARTH.
THE SPIRIT OF THE MOON.
SPIRITS OF THE HOURS.
SPIRITS. ECHOES. FAUNS. FURIES.

# PROMETHEUS UNBOUND

## ACT 1.

**SCENE: A RAVINE OF ICY ROCKS IN THE INDIAN CAUCASUS. PROMETHEUS IS DISCOVERED BOUND TO THE PRECIPICE. PANTEA AND IONE ARE SEATED AT HIS FEET. TIME: NIGHT. DURING THE SCENE, MORNING SLOWLY BREAKS.**

PROMETHEUS:
Monarch of Gods and Daemons, and all Spirits
But One, who throng those bright and rolling worlds
Which Thou and I alone of living things
Behold with sleepless eyes! regard this Earth
Made multitudinous with thy slaves, whom thou          5
Requitest for knee-worship, prayer, and praise,
And toil, and hecatombs of broken hearts,
With fear and self-contempt and barren hope.
Whilst me, who am thy foe, eyeless in hate,
Hast thou made reign and triumph, to thy scorn,          10
O'er mine own misery and thy vain revenge.
Three thousand years of sleep-unsheltered hours,
And moments aye divided by keen pangs
Till they seemed years, torture and solitude,
Scorn and despair—these are mine empire—          15
More glorious far than that which thou surveyest
From thine unenvied throne, O Mighty God!
Almighty, had I deigned to share the shame
Of thine ill tyranny, and hung not here
Nailed to this wall of eagle-baffling mountain,          20
Black, wintry, dead, unmeasured; without herb,
Insect, or beast, or shape or sound of life.
Ah me! alas, pain, pain ever, for ever!
No change, no pause, no hope! Yet I endure.
I ask the Earth, have not the mountains felt?          25
I ask yon Heaven, the all-beholding Sun,
Has it not seen? The Sea, in storm or calm,
Heaven's ever-changing Shadow, spread below,
Have its deaf waves not heard my agony?
Ah me! alas, pain, pain ever, for ever!          30
The crawling glaciers pierce me with the spears

Of their moon-freezing crystals; the bright chains
Eat with their burning cold into my bones.
Heaven's winged hound, polluting from thy lips
His beak in poison not his own, tears up                                    35
My heart; and shapeless sights come wandering by,
The ghastly people of the realm of dream,
Mocking me: and the Earthquake-fiends are charged
To wrench the rivets from my quivering wounds
When the rocks split and close again behind:                                40
While from their loud abysses howling throng
The genii of the storm, urging the rage
Of whirlwind, and afflict me with keen hail.
And yet to me welcome is day and night,
Whether one breaks the hoar-frost of the morn,                              45
Or starry, dim, and slow, the other climbs
The leaden-coloured east; for then they lead
The wingless, crawling hours, one among whom
—As some dark Priest hales the reluctant victim—
Shall drag thee, cruel King, to kiss the blood                              50
From these pale feet, which then might trample thee
If they disdained not such a prostrate slave.
Disdain! Ah, no! I pity thee. What ruin
Will hunt thee undefended through wide Heaven!
How will thy soul, cloven to its depth with terror,                         55
Gape like a hell within! I speak in grief,
Not exultation, for I hate no more,
As then ere misery made me wise. The curse
Once breathed on thee I would recall. Ye Mountains,
Whose many-voiced Echoes, through the mist                                  60
Of cataracts, flung the thunder of that spell!
Ye icy Springs, stagnant with wrinkling frost,
Which vibrated to hear me, and then crept
Shuddering through India! Thou serenest Air,
Through which the Sun walks burning without beams!                          65
And ye swift Whirlwinds, who on poised wings
Hung mute and moveless o'er yon hushed abyss,
As thunder, louder than your own, made rock
The orbed world! If then my words had power,
Though I am changed so that aught evil wish                                 70
Is dead within; although no memory be
Of what is hate, let them not lose it now!
What was that curse? for ye all heard me speak.

FIRST VOICE (FROM THE MOUNTAINS):
Thrice three hundred thousand years
O'er the Earthquake's couch we stood: 75
Oft, as men convulsed with fears,
We trembled in our multitude.

SECOND VOICE (FROM THE SPRINGS):
Thunderbolts had parched our water,
We had been stained with bitter blood,
And had run mute, 'mid shrieks of slaughter, 80
Thro' a city and a solitude.

THIRD VOICE (FROM THE AIR):
I had clothed, since Earth uprose,
Its wastes in colours not their own,
And oft had my serene repose
Been cloven by many a rending groan. 85

FOURTH VOICE (FROM THE WHIRLWINDS):
We had soared beneath these mountains
Unresting ages; nor had thunder,
Nor yon volcano's flaming fountains,
Nor any power above or under
Ever made us mute with wonder. 90

FIRST VOICE:
But never bowed our snowy crest
As at the voice of thine unrest.

SECOND VOICE:
Never such a sound before
To the Indian waves we bore.
A pilot asleep on the howling sea 95
Leaped up from the deck in agony,
And heard, and cried, 'Ah, woe is me!'
And died as mad as the wild waves be.

THIRD VOICE:
By such dread words from Earth to Heaven
My still realm was never riven: 100
When its wound was closed, there stood
Darkness o'er the day like blood.

FOURTH VOICE:
And we shrank back: for dreams of ruin
To frozen caves our flight pursuing
Made us keep silence—thus—and thus—                                105
Though silence is a hell to us.

THE EARTH:
The tongueless caverns of the craggy hills
Cried, 'Misery!' then; the hollow Heaven replied,
'Misery!' And the Ocean's purple waves,
Climbing the land, howled to the lashing winds,                     110
And the pale nations heard it, 'Misery!'

PROMETHEUS:
I hear a sound of voices: not the voice
Which I gave forth. Mother, thy sons and thou
Scorn him, without whose all-enduring will
Beneath the fierce omnipotence of Jove,                             115
Both they and thou had vanished, like thin mist
Unrolled on the morning wind. Know ye not me,
The Titan? He who made his agony
The barrier to your else all-conquering foe?
Oh, rock-embosomed lawns, and snow-fed streams,                     120
Now seen athwart frore vapours, deep below,
Through whose o'ershadowing woods I wandered once
With Asia, drinking life from her loved eyes;
Why scorns the spirit which informs ye, now
To commune with me? me alone, who checked,                          125
As one who checks a fiend-drawn charioteer,
The falsehood and the force of him who reigns
Supreme, and with the groans of pining slaves
Fills your dim glens and liquid wildernesses:
Why answer ye not, still? Brethren!

THE EARTH:
They dare not.                                                      130

PROMETHEUS:
Who dares? for I would hear that curse again.
Ha, what an awful whisper rises up!
'Tis scarce like sound: it tingles through the frame
As lightning tingles, hovering ere it strike.

Speak, Spirit! from thine inorganic voice                    135
I only know that thou art moving near
And love. How cursed I him?

THE EARTH:
How canst thou hear
Who knowest not the language of the dead?

PROMETHEUS:
Thou art a living spirit; speak as they.

THE EARTH:
I dare not speak like life, lest Heaven's fell King          140
Should hear, and link me to some wheel of pain
More torturing than the one whereon I roll.
Subtle thou art and good; and though the Gods
Hear not this voice, yet thou art more than God,
Being wise and kind: earnestly hearken now.                  145

PROMETHEUS:
Obscurely through my brain, like shadows dim,
Sweep awful thoughts, rapid and thick. I feel
Faint, like one mingled in entwining love;
Yet 'tis not pleasure.

THE EARTH:
No, thou canst not hear:
Thou art immortal, and this tongue is known                  150
Only to those who die.

PROMETHEUS:
And what art thou,
O, melancholy Voice?

THE EARTH:
I am the Earth,
Thy mother; she within whose stony veins,
To the last fibre of the loftiest tree
Whose thin leaves trembled in the frozen air,                155
Joy ran, as blood within a living frame,
When thou didst from her bosom, like a cloud
Of glory, arise, a spirit of keen joy!

And at thy voice her pining sons uplifted
Their prostrate brows from the polluting dust,                    160
And our almighty Tyrant with fierce dread
Grew pale, until his thunder chained thee here.
Then, see those million worlds which burn and roll
Around us: their inhabitants beheld
My sphered light wane in wide Heaven; the sea                     165
Was lifted by strange tempest, and new fire
From earthquake-rifted mountains of bright snow
Shook its portentous hair beneath Heaven's frown;
Lightning and Inundation vexed the plains;
Blue thistles bloomed in cities; foodless toads                  170
Within voluptuous chambers panting crawled:
When Plague had fallen on man, and beast, and worm,
And Famine; and black blight on herb and tree;
And in the corn, and vines, and meadow-grass,
Teemed ineradicable poisonous weeds                              175
Draining their growth, for my wan breast was dry
With grief; and the thin air, my breath, was stained
With the contagion of a mother's hate
Breathed on her child's destroyer; ay, I heard
Thy curse, the which, if thou rememberest not,                   180
Yet my innumerable seas and streams,
Mountains, and caves, and winds, and yon wide air,
And the inarticulate people of the dead,
Preserve, a treasured spell. We meditate
In secret joy and hope those dreadful words,                     185
But dare not speak them.

PROMETHEUS:
Venerable mother!
All else who live and suffer take from thee
Some comfort; flowers, and fruits, and happy sounds,
And love, though fleeting; these may not be mine.
But mine own words, I pray, deny me not.                         190

THE EARTH:
They shall be told. Ere Babylon was dust,
The Magus Zoroaster, my dead child,
Met his own image walking in the garden.
That apparition, sole of men, he saw.
For know there are two worlds of life and death:                 195

One that which thou beholdest; but the other
Is underneath the grave, where do inhabit
The shadows of all forms that think and live
Till death unite them and they part no more;
Dreams and the light imaginings of men,                    200
And all that faith creates or love desires,
Terrible, strange, sublime and beauteous shapes.
There thou art, and dost hang, a writhing shade,
'Mid whirlwind-peopled mountains; all the gods
Are there, and all the powers of nameless worlds,          205
Vast, sceptred phantoms; heroes, men, and beasts;
And Demogorgon, a tremendous gloom;
And he, the supreme Tyrant, on his throne
Of burning gold. Son, one of these shall utter
The curse which all remember. Call at will                 210
Thine own ghost, or the ghost of Jupiter,
Hades or Typhon, or what mightier Gods
From all-prolific Evil, since thy ruin,
Have sprung, and trampled on my prostrate sons.
Ask, and they must reply: so the revenge                   215
Of the Supreme may sweep through vacant shades,
As rainy wind through the abandoned gate
Of a fallen palace.

PROMETHEUS:
Mother, let not aught
Of that which may be evil, pass again
My lips, or those of aught resembling me.                  220
Phantasm of Jupiter, arise, appear!

IONE:
My wings are folded o'er mine ears:
My wings are crossed o'er mine eyes:
Yet through their silver shade appears,
And through their lulling plumes arise,                    225
A Shape, a throng of sounds;
May it be no ill to thee
O thou of many wounds!
Near whom, for our sweet sister's sake,
Ever thus we watch and wake.                               230

PANTHEA:
The sound is of whirlwind underground,
Earthquake, and fire, and mountains cloven;
The shape is awful like the sound,
Clothed in dark purple, star-inwoven.
A sceptre of pale gold                                                    235
To stay steps proud, o'er the slow cloud
His veined hand doth hold.
Cruel he looks, but calm and strong,
Like one who does, not suffers wrong.

PHANTASM OF JUPITER:
Why have the secret powers of this strange world                          240
Driven me, a frail and empty phantom, hither
On direst storms? What unaccustomed sounds
Are hovering on my lips, unlike the voice
With which our pallid race hold ghastly talk
In darkness? And, proud sufferer, who art thou?                           245

PROMETHEUS:
Tremendous Image, as thou art must be
He whom thou shadowest forth. I am his foe,
The Titan. Speak the words which I would hear,
Although no thought inform thine empty voice.

THE EARTH:
Listen! And though your echoes must be mute,                              250
Grey mountains, and old woods, and haunted springs,
Prophetic caves, and isle-surrounding streams,
Rejoice to hear what yet ye cannot speak.

PHANTASM:
A spirit seizes me and speaks within:
It tears me as fire tears a thunder-cloud.                                255

PANTHEA:
See, how he lifts his mighty looks, the Heaven
Darkens above.

IONE:
He speaks! O shelter me!

PROMETHEUS:
I see the curse on gestures proud and cold,
And looks of firm defiance, and calm hate,
And such despair as mocks itself with smiles,                    260
Written as on a scroll: yet speak! Oh, speak!

PHANTASM:
Fiend, I defy thee! with a calm, fixed mind,
All that thou canst inflict I bid thee do;
Foul Tyrant both of Gods and Humankind,
One only being shalt thou not subdue.                            265
Rain then thy plagues upon me here,
Ghastly disease, and frenzying fear;
And let alternate frost and fire
Eat into me, and be thine ire
Lightning, and cutting hail, and legioned forms                  270
Of furies, driving by upon the wounding storms.

Ay, do thy worst. Thou art omnipotent.
O'er all things but thyself I gave thee power,
And my own will. Be thy swift mischiefs sent
To blast mankind, from yon ethereal tower.                       275
Let thy malignant spirit move
In darkness over those I love:
On me and mine I imprecate
The utmost torture of thy hate;
And thus devote to sleepless agony,                              280
This undeclining head while thou must reign on high.

But thou, who art the God and Lord: O, thou,
Who fillest with thy soul this world of woe,
To whom all things of Earth and Heaven do bow
In fear and worship: all-prevailing foe!                         285
I curse thee! let a sufferer's curse
Clasp thee, his torturer, like remorse;
Till thine Infinity shall be
A robe of envenomed agony;
And thine Omnipotence a crown of pain,                           290
To cling like burning gold round thy dissolving brain.

Heap on thy soul, by virtue of this Curse,
Ill deeds, then be thou damned, beholding good;

Both infinite as is the universe,
And thou, and thy self-torturing solitude.                    295
An awful image of calm power
Though now thou sittest, let the hour
Come, when thou must appear to be
That which thou art internally;
And after many a false and fruitless crime                    300
Scorn track thy lagging fall through boundless space and time.

PROMETHEUS:
Were these my words, O Parent?

THE EARTH:
They were thine.

PROMETHEUS:
It doth repent me: words are quick and vain;
Grief for awhile is blind, and so was mine.
I wish no living thing to suffer pain.                         305

THE EARTH:
Misery, Oh misery to me,
That Jove at length should vanquish thee.
Wail, howl aloud, Land and Sea,
The Earth's rent heart shall answer ye.
Howl, Spirits of the living and the dead,                     310
Your refuge, your defence, lies fallen and vanquished.

FIRST ECHO:
Lies fallen and vanquished!

SECOND ECHO:
Fallen and vanquished!

IONE:
Fear not: 'tis but some passing spasm,
The Titan is unvanquished still.                              315
But see, where through the azure chasm
Of yon forked and snowy hill
Trampling the slant winds on high
With golden-sandalled feet, that glow
Under plumes of purple dye,                                   320

Like rose-ensanguined ivory,
A Shape comes now,
Stretching on high from his right hand
A serpent-cinctured wand.

PANTHEA:
'Tis Jove's world-wandering herald, Mercury.                    325

IONE:
And who are those with hydra tresses
And iron wings that climb the wind,
Whom the frowning God represses
Like vapours steaming up behind,
Clanging loud, an endless crowd—                    330

PANTHEA:
These are Jove's tempest-walking hounds,
Whom he gluts with groans and blood,
When charioted on sulphurous cloud
He bursts Heaven's bounds.

IONE:
Are they now led, from the thin dead                    335
On new pangs to be fed?

PANTHEA:
The Titan looks as ever, firm, not proud.

FIRST FURY:
Ha! I scent life!

SECOND FURY:
Let me but look into his eyes!

THIRD FURY:
The hope of torturing him smells like a heap
Of corpses, to a death-bird after battle.                    340

FIRST FURY:
Darest thou delay, O Herald! take cheer, Hounds
Of Hell: what if the Son of Maia soon
Should make us food and sport—who can please long

The Omnipotent?

MERCURY:
Back to your towers of iron,
And gnash, beside the streams of fire and wail,                345
Your foodless teeth. Geryon, arise! and Gorgon,
Chimaera, and thou Sphinx, subtlest of fiends
Who ministered to Thebes Heaven's poisoned wine,
Unnatural love, and more unnatural hate:
These shall perform your task.

FIRST FURY:
Oh, mercy! mercy!                                             350
We die with our desire: drive us not back!

MERCURY:
Crouch then in silence.
Awful Sufferer!
To thee unwilling, most unwillingly
I come, by the great Father's will driven down,
To execute a doom of new revenge.                            355
Alas! I pity thee, and hate myself
That I can do no more: aye from thy sight
Returning, for a season, Heaven seems Hell,
So thy worn form pursues me night and day,
Smiling reproach. Wise art thou, firm and good,             360
But vainly wouldst stand forth alone in strife
Against the Omnipotent; as yon clear lamps
That measure and divide the weary years
From which there is no refuge, long have taught
And long must teach. Even now thy Torturer arms             365
With the strange might of unimagined pains
The powers who scheme slow agonies in Hell,
And my commission is to lead them here,
Or what more subtle, foul, or savage fiends
People the abyss, and leave them to their task.             370
Be it not so! there is a secret known
To thee, and to none else of living things,
Which may transfer the sceptre of wide Heaven,
The fear of which perplexes the Supreme:
Clothe it in words, and bid it clasp his throne             375
In intercession; bend thy soul in prayer,

And like a suppliant in some gorgeous fane,
Let the will kneel within thy haughty heart:
For benefits and meek submission tame
The fiercest and the mightiest.

PROMETHEUS:
Evil minds                                                                380
Change good to their own nature. I gave all
He has; and in return he chains me here
Years, ages, night and day: whether the Sun
Split my parched skin, or in the moony night
The crystal-winged snow cling round my hair:            385
Whilst my beloved race is trampled down
By his thought-executing ministers.
Such is the tyrant's recompense: 'tis just:
He who is evil can receive no good;
And for a world bestowed, or a friend lost,                 390
He can feel hate, fear, shame; not gratitude:
He but requites me for his own misdeed.
Kindness to such is keen reproach, which breaks
With bitter stings the light sleep of Revenge.
Submission, thou dost know I cannot try:                    395
For what submission but that fatal word,
The death-seal of mankind's captivity,
Like the Sicilian's hair-suspended sword,
Which trembles o'er his crown, would he accept,
Or could I yield? Which yet I will not yield.               400
Let others flatter Crime, where it sits throned
In brief Omnipotence: secure are they:
For Justice, when triumphant, will weep down
Pity, not punishment, on her own wrongs,
Too much avenged by those who err. I wait,               405
Enduring thus, the retributive hour
Which since we spake is even nearer now.
But hark, the hell-hounds clamour: fear delay:
Behold! Heaven lowers under thy Father's frown.

MERCURY:
Oh, that we might be spared; I to inflict                      410
And thou to suffer! Once more answer me:
Thou knowest not the period of Jove's power?

PROMETHEUS:
I know but this, that it must come.

MERCURY:
Alas!
Thou canst not count thy years to come of pain?

PROMETHEUS:
They last while Jove must reign: nor more, nor less　　　415
Do I desire or fear.

MERCURY:
Yet pause, and plunge
Into Eternity, where recorded time,
Even all that we imagine, age on age,
Seems but a point, and the reluctant mind
Flags wearily in its unending flight,　　　420
Till it sink, dizzy, blind, lost, shelterless;
Perchance it has not numbered the slow years
Which thou must spend in torture, unreprieved?

PROMETHEUS:
Perchance no thought can count them, yet they pass.

MERCURY:
If thou might'st dwell among the Gods the while
Lapped in voluptuous joy?　　　425

PROMETHEUS:
I would not quit
This bleak ravine, these unrepentant pains.

MERCURY:
Alas! I wonder at, yet pity thee.

PROMETHEUS:
Pity the self-despising slaves of Heaven,
Not me, within whose mind sits peace serene.　　　430
As light in the sun, throned: how vain is talk!
Call up the fiends.

IONE:
O, sister, look! White fire
Has cloven to the roots yon huge snow-loaded cedar;
How fearfully God's thunder howls behind!

MERCURY:
I must obey his words and thine: alas!                    435
Most heavily remorse hangs at my heart!

PANTHEA:
See where the child of Heaven, with winged feet,
Runs down the slanted sunlight of the dawn.

IONE:
Dear sister, close thy plumes over thine eyes
Lest thou behold and die: they come: they come                    440
Blackening the birth of day with countless wings,
And hollow underneath, like death.

FIRST FURY:
Prometheus!

SECOND FURY:
Immortal Titan!

THIRD FURY:
Champion of Heaven's slaves!

PROMETHEUS:
He whom some dreadful voice invokes is here,
Prometheus, the chained Titan. Horrible forms,                    445
What and who are ye? Never yet there came
Phantasms so foul through monster-teeming Hell
From the all-miscreative brain of Jove;
Whilst I behold such execrable shapes,
Methinks I grow like what I contemplate,                    450
And laugh and stare in loathsome sympathy.

P dislikes furies but thinks he becomes like one

FIRST FURY:
We are the ministers of pain, and fear,
And disappointment, and mistrust, and hate,
And clinging crime; and as lean dogs pursue

furies are part of pain to world

Through wood and lake some struck and sobbing fawn,                    455
We track all things that weep, and bleed, and live,
When the great King betrays them to our will.

PROMETHEUS:                    *Furios*
Oh! many fearful natures in one name,
I know ye; and these lakes and echoes know
The darkness and the clangour of your wings.                    460
But why more hideous than your loathed selves
Gather ye up in legions from the deep?

SECOND FURY:
We knew not that: Sisters, rejoice, rejoice!

PROMETHEUS:
Can aught exult in its deformity?

SECOND FURY:
The beauty of delight makes lovers glad,                    465
Gazing on one another: so are we.
As from the rose which the pale priestess kneels
To gather for her festal crown of flowers
The aereal crimson falls, flushing her cheek,
So from our victim's destined agony                    470
The shade which is our form invests us round,
Else we are shapeless as our mother Night.

PROMETHEUS:
I laugh your power, and his who sent you here,
To lowest scorn. Pour forth the cup of pain.

FIRST FURY:
Thou thinkest we will rend thee bone from bone,                    475
And nerve from nerve, working like fire within?

PROMETHEUS:
Pain is my element, as hate is thine;
Ye rend me now; I care not.

SECOND FURY:
Dost imagine
We will but laugh into thy lidless eyes?

PROMETHEUS:
I weigh not what ye do, but what ye suffer,                    480
Being evil. Cruel was the power which called
You, or aught else so wretched, into light.

THIRD FURY:
Thou think'st we will live through thee, one by one,
Like animal life, and though we can obscure not
The soul which burns within, that we will dwell               485
Beside it, like a vain loud multitude
Vexing the self-content of wisest men:
That we will be dread thought beneath thy brain,
And foul desire round thine astonished heart,
And blood within thy labyrinthine veins                       490
Crawling like agony?

PROMETHEUS:
Why, ye are thus now;
Yet am I king over myself, and rule
The torturing and conflicting throngs within,
As Jove rules you when Hell grows mutinous.

CHORUS OF FURIES:
From the ends of the earth, from the ends of the earth,       495
Where the night has its grave and the morning its birth,
Come, come, come!
Oh, ye who shake hills with the scream of your mirth,
When cities sink howling in ruin; and ye
Who with wingless footsteps trample the sea,                  500
And close upon Shipwreck and Famine's track,
Sit chattering with joy on the foodless wreck;
Come, come, come!
Leave the bed, low, cold, and red,
Strewed beneath a nation dead;                                505
Leave the hatred, as in ashes
Fire is left for future burning:
It will burst in bloodier flashes
When ye stir it, soon returning:
Leave the self-contempt implanted                             510
In young spirits, sense-enchanted,
Misery's yet unkindled fuel:
Leave Hell's secrets half unchanted

To the maniac dreamer; cruel
More than ye can be with hate                          515
Is he with fear.
Come, come, come!
We are steaming up from Hell's wide gate
And we burthen the blast of the atmosphere,
But vainly we toil till ye come here.                  520

IONE:
Sister, I hear the thunder of new wings.

PANTHEA:
These solid mountains quiver with the sound
Even as the tremulous air: their shadows make
The space within my plumes more black than night.

FIRST FURY:
Your call was as a winged car,                         525
Driven on whirlwinds fast and far;
It rapped us from red gulfs of war.

SECOND FURY:
From wide cities, famine-wasted;

THIRD FURY:
Groans half heard, and blood untasted;

FOURTH FURY:
Kingly conclaves stern and cold,                       530
Where blood with gold is bought and sold;

FIFTH FURY:
From the furnace, white and hot,
In which—

A FURY:
Speak not: whisper not:
I know all that ye would tell,
But to speak might break the spell                     535
Which must bend the Invincible,
The stern of thought;
He yet defies the deepest power of Hell.

FURY:
Tear the veil!

ANOTHER FURY:
It is torn.

CHORUS:
The pale stars of the morn
Shine on a misery, dire to be borne.                              540
Dost thou faint, mighty Titan? We laugh thee to scorn.
Dost thou boast the clear knowledge thou waken'dst for man?
Then was kindled within him a thirst which outran
Those perishing waters; a thirst of fierce fever,
Hope, love, doubt, desire, which consume him for ever.            545
One came forth of gentle worth
Smiling on the sanguine earth;
His words outlived him, like swift poison
Withering up truth, peace, and pity.
Look! where round the wide horizon                                550
Many a million-peopled city
Vomits smoke in the bright air.
Mark that outcry of despair!
'Tis his mild and gentle ghost
Wailing for the faith he kindled:                                 555
Look again, the flames almost
To a glow-worm's lamp have dwindled:
The survivors round the embers
Gather in dread.
Joy, joy, joy!                                                    560
Past ages crowd on thee, but each one remembers,
And the future is dark, and the present is spread
Like a pillow of thorns for thy slumberless head.

SEMICHORUS 1:
Drops of bloody agony flow
From his white and quivering brow.                                565
Grant a little respite now:
See a disenchanted nation
Springs like day from desolation;
To Truth its state is dedicate,
And Freedom leads it forth, her mate;                             570
A legioned band of linked brothers

Whom Love calls children—

SEMICHORUS 2:
'Tis another's:
See how kindred murder kin:
'Tis the vintage-time for death and sin:
Blood, like new wine, bubbles within:　　　　　　　575
Till Despair smothers
The struggling world, which slaves and tyrants win.

[ALL THE FURIES VANISH, EXCEPT ONE.]

IONE:
Hark, sister! what a low yet dreadful groan
Quite unsuppressed is tearing up the heart
Of the good Titan, as storms tear the deep,　　　　　580
And beasts hear the sea moan in inland caves.
Darest thou observe how the fiends torture him?

PANTHEA:
Alas! I looked forth twice, but will no more.

IONE:
What didst thou see?

PANTHEA:
A woeful sight: a youth
With patient looks nailed to a crucifix.　　　　　　585

IONE:
What next?

PANTHEA:
The heaven around, the earth below
Was peopled with thick shapes of human death,
All horrible, and wrought by human hands,
And some appeared the work of human hearts,
For men were slowly killed by frowns and smiles:　　590
And other sights too foul to speak and live
Were wandering by. Let us not tempt worse fear
By looking forth: those groans are grief enough.

FURY:
Behold an emblem: those who do endure
Deep wrongs for man, and scorn, and chains, but heap          595
Thousand-fold torment on themselves and him.

PROMETHEUS:
Remit the anguish of that lighted stare;
Close those wan lips; let that thorn-wounded brow
Stream not with blood; it mingles with thy tears!
Fix, fix those tortured orbs in peace and death,             600
So thy sick throes shake not that crucifix,
So those pale fingers play not with thy gore.
O, horrible! Thy name I will not speak,
It hath become a curse. I see, I see
The wise, the mild, the lofty, and the just,                 605
Whom thy slaves hate for being like to thee,
Some hunted by foul lies from their heart's home,
An early-chosen, late-lamented home;
As hooded ounces cling to the driven hind;
Some linked to corpses in unwholesome cells:                 610
Some—Hear I not the multitude laugh loud?—
Impaled in lingering fire: and mighty realms
Float by my feet, like sea-uprooted isles,
Whose sons are kneaded down in common blood
By the red light of their own burning homes.                 615

FURY:
Blood thou canst see, and fire; and canst hear groans;
Worse things unheard, unseen, remain behind.

PROMETHEUS:
Worse?

FURY:
In each human heart terror survives
The ruin it has gorged: the loftiest fear
All that they would disdain to think were true:              620
Hypocrisy and custom make their minds
The fanes of many a worship, now outworn.
They dare not devise good for man's estate,
And yet they know not that they do not dare.
The good want power, but to weep barren tears.               625

The powerful goodness want: worse need for them.
The wise want love; and those who love want wisdom;
And all best things are thus confused to ill.
Many are strong and rich, and would be just,
But live among their suffering fellow-men                    630
As if none felt: they know not what they do.

PROMETHEUS:
Thy words are like a cloud of winged snakes;
And yet I pity those they torture not.

FURY:
Thou pitiest them? I speak no more!
[VANISHES.]

PROMETHEUS:
Ah woe!
Ah woe! Alas! pain, pain ever, for ever!                     635
I close my tearless eyes, but see more clear
Thy works within my woe-illumed mind,
Thou subtle tyrant! Peace is in the grave.
The grave hides all things beautiful and good:
I am a God and cannot find it there,                         640
Nor would I seek it: for, though dread revenge,
This is defeat, fierce king, not victory.
The sights with which thou torturest gird my soul
With new endurance, till the hour arrives
When they shall be no types of things which are.             645

PANTHEA:
Alas! what sawest thou more?

PROMETHEUS:
There are two woes:
To speak, and to behold; thou spare me one.
Names are there, Nature's sacred watchwords, they
Were borne aloft in bright emblazonry;
The nations thronged around, and cried aloud,                650
As with one voice, Truth, liberty, and love!
Suddenly fierce confusion fell from heaven
Among them: there was strife, deceit, and fear:
Tyrants rushed in, and did divide the spoil.

This was the shadow of the truth I saw. 655

THE EARTH:
I felt thy torture, son; with such mixed joy
As pain and virtue give. To cheer thy state
I bid ascend those subtle and fair spirits,
Whose homes are the dim caves of human thought,
And who inhabit, as birds wing the wind, 660
Its world-surrounding aether: they behold
Beyond that twilight realm, as in a glass,
The future: may they speak comfort to thee!

PANTHEA:
Look, sister, where a troop of spirits gather,
Like flocks of clouds in spring's delightful weather, 665
Thronging in the blue air!

IONE:
And see! more come,
Like fountain-vapours when the winds are dumb,
That climb up the ravine in scattered lines.
And, hark! is it the music of the pines?
Is it the lake? Is it the waterfall? 670

PANTHEA:
'Tis something sadder, sweeter far than all.

CHORUS OF SPIRITS:
From unremembered ages we
Gentle guides and guardians be
Of heaven-oppressed mortality;
And we breathe, and sicken not, 675
The atmosphere of human thought:
Be it dim, and dank, and gray,
Like a storm-extinguished day,
Travelled o'er by dying gleams;
Be it bright as all between 680
Cloudless skies and windless streams,
Silent, liquid, and serene;
As the birds within the wind,
As the fish within the wave,
As the thoughts of man's own mind 685

Float through all above the grave;
We make there our liquid lair,
Voyaging cloudlike and unpent
Through the boundless element:
Thence we bear the prophecy                                    690
Which begins and ends in thee!

IONE:
More yet come, one by one: the air around them
Looks radiant as the air around a star.

FIRST SPIRIT:
On a battle-trumpet's blast
I fled hither, fast, fast, fast,                                695
'Mid the darkness upward cast.
From the dust of creeds outworn,
From the tyrant's banner torn,
Gathering 'round me, onward borne,
There was mingled many a cry—                                  700
Freedom! Hope! Death! Victory!
Till they faded through the sky;
And one sound, above, around,
One sound beneath, around, above,
Was moving; 'twas the soul of Love;                            705
'Twas the hope, the prophecy,
Which begins and ends in thee.

SECOND SPIRIT:
A rainbow's arch stood on the sea,
Which rocked beneath, immovably;
And the triumphant storm did flee,                             710
Like a conqueror, swift and proud,
Between, with many a captive cloud,
A shapeless, dark and rapid crowd,
Each by lightning riven in half:
I heard the thunder hoarsely laugh:                            715
Mighty fleets were strewn like chaff
And spread beneath a hell of death
O'er the white waters. I alit
On a great ship lightning-split,
And speeded hither on the sigh                                 720
Of one who gave an enemy

His plank, then plunged aside to die.

THIRD SPIRIT:
I sate beside a sage's bed,
And the lamp was burning red
Near the book where he had fed,                            725
When a Dream with plumes of flame,
To his pillow hovering came,
And I knew it was the same
Which had kindled long ago
Pity, eloquence, and woe;                                   730
And the world awhile below
Wore the shade, its lustre made.
It has borne me here as fleet
As Desire's lightning feet:
I must ride it back ere morrow,                             735
Or the sage will wake in sorrow.

FOURTH SPIRIT:
On a poet's lips I slept
Dreaming like a love-adept
In the sound his breathing kept;
Nor seeks nor finds he mortal blisses,                      740
But feeds on the aereal kisses
Of shapes that haunt thought's wildernesses.
He will watch from dawn to gloom
The lake-reflected sun illume
The yellow bees in the ivy-bloom,                           745
Nor heed nor see, what things they be;
But from these create he can
Forms more real than living man,
Nurslings of immortality!
One of these awakened me,                                   750
And I sped to succour thee.

IONE:
Behold'st thou not two shapes from the east and west
Come, as two doves to one beloved nest,
Twin nurslings of the all-sustaining air
On swift still wings glide down the atmosphere?            755
And, hark! their sweet sad voices! 'tis despair
Mingled with love and then dissolved in sound.

PANTHEA:
Canst thou speak, sister? all my words are drowned.

IONE:
Their beauty gives me voice. See how they float
On their sustaining wings of skiey grain,                              760
Orange and azure deepening into gold:
Their soft smiles light the air like a star's fire.

CHORUS OF SPIRITS:
Hast thou beheld the form of Love?

FIFTH SPIRIT:
As over wide dominions
I sped, like some swift cloud that wings the wide air's wildernesses,
That planet-crested shape swept by on lightning-braided pinions,    765
Scattering the liquid joy of life from his ambrosial tresses:
His footsteps paved the world with light; but as I passed 'twas fading,
And hollow Ruin yawned behind: great sages bound in madness,
And headless patriots, and pale youths who perished, unupbraiding,
Gleamed in the night. I wandered o'er, till thou, O King of sadness, 770
Turned by thy smile the worst I saw to recollected gladness.

SIXTH SPIRIT:
Ah, sister! Desolation is a delicate thing:
It walks not on the earth, it floats not on the air,
But treads with lulling footstep, and fans with silent wing
The tender hopes which in their hearts the best and gentlest bear;   775
Who, soothed to false repose by the fanning plumes above
And the music-stirring motion of its soft and busy feet,
Dream visions of aereal joy, and call the monster, Love,
And wake, and find the shadow Pain, as he whom now we greet.

CHORUS:
Though Ruin now Love's shadow be,                                    780
Following him, destroyingly,
On Death's white and winged steed,
Which the fleetest cannot flee,
Trampling down both flower and weed,
Man and beast, and foul and fair,                                   785
Like a tempest through the air;
Thou shalt quell this horseman grim,

Woundless though in heart or limb.

PROMETHEUS:
Spirits! how know ye this shall be?

CHORUS:
In the atmosphere we breathe,                                    790
As buds grow red when the snow-storms flee,
From Spring gathering up beneath,
Whose mild winds shake the elder-brake,
And the wandering herdsmen know
That the white-thorn soon will blow:                             795
Wisdom, Justice, Love, and Peace,
When they struggle to increase,
Are to us as soft winds be
To shepherd boys, the prophecy
Which begins and ends in thee.                                   800

IONE:
Where are the Spirits fled?

PANTHEA:
Only a sense
Remains of them, like the omnipotence
Of music, when the inspired voice and lute
Languish, ere yet the responses are mute,
Which through the deep and labyrinthine soul,                    805
Like echoes through long caverns, wind and roll.

PROMETHEUS:
How fair these airborn shapes! and yet I feel
Most vain all hope but love; and thou art far,
Asia! who, when my being overflowed,
Wert like a golden chalice to bright wine                        810
Which else had sunk into the thirsty dust.
All things are still: alas! how heavily
This quiet morning weighs upon my heart;
Though I should dream I could even sleep with grief
If slumber were denied not. I would fain                         815
Be what it is my destiny to be,
The saviour and the strength of suffering man,
Or sink into the original gulf of things:

There is no agony, and no solace left;
Earth can console, Heaven can torment no more.                    820

PANTHEA:
Hast thou forgotten one who watches thee
The cold dark night, and never sleeps but when
The shadow of thy spirit falls on her?

PROMETHEUS:
I said all hope was vain but love: thou lovest.

PANTHEA:
Deeply in truth; but the eastern star looks white,               825
And Asia waits in that far Indian vale,
The scene of her sad exile; rugged once
And desolate and frozen, like this ravine;
But now invested with fair flowers and herbs,
And haunted by sweet airs and sounds, which flow                 830
Among the woods and waters, from the aether
Of her transforming presence, which would fade
If it were mingled not with thine. Farewell!

## ACT 2.

### SCENE 2.1: MORNING.
### A LOVELY VALE IN THE INDIAN CAUCASUS.
### ASIA, ALONE.

ASIA:
From all the blasts of heaven thou hast descended:
Yes, like a spirit, like a thought, which makes
Unwonted tears throng to the horny eyes,
And beatings haunt the desolated heart,
Which should have learnt repose: thou hast descended               5
Cradled in tempests; thou dost wake, O Spring!
O child of many winds! As suddenly
Thou comest as the memory of a dream,
Which now is sad because it hath been sweet;
Like genius, or like joy which riseth up                          10
As from the earth, clothing with golden clouds
The desert of our life.

This is the season, this the day, the hour;
At sunrise thou shouldst come, sweet sister mine,
Too long desired, too long delaying, come!                    15
How like death-worms the wingless moments crawl!
The point of one white star is quivering still
Deep in the orange light of widening morn
Beyond the purple mountains: through a chasm
Of wind-divided mist the darker lake                          20
Reflects it: now it wanes: it gleams again
As the waves fade, and as the burning threads
Of woven cloud unravel in pale air:
'Tis lost! and through yon peaks of cloud-like snow
The roseate sunlight quivers: hear I not                      25
The Aeolian music of her sea-green plumes
Winnowing the crimson dawn?

PANTHEA [ENTERS]:
I feel, I see
Those eyes which burn through smiles that fade in tears,
Like stars half quenched in mists of silver dew.
Beloved and most beautiful, who wearest                       30
The shadow of that soul by which I live,
How late thou art! the sphered sun had climbed
The sea; my heart was sick with hope, before
The printless air felt thy belated plumes.

PANTHEA:
Pardon, great Sister! but my wings were faint                 35
With the delight of a remembered dream,
As are the noontide plumes of summer winds
Satiate with sweet flowers. I was wont to sleep
Peacefully, and awake refreshed and calm
Before the sacred Titan's fall, and thy                       40
Unhappy love, had made, through use and pity,
Both love and woe familiar to my heart
As they had grown to thine: erewhile I slept
Under the glaucous caverns of old Ocean
Within dim bowers of green and purple moss,                   45
Our young Ione's soft and milky arms
Locked then, as now, behind my dark, moist hair,
While my shut eyes and cheek were pressed within
The folded depth of her life-breathing bosom:

But not as now, since I am made the wind                         50
Which fails beneath the music that I bear
Of thy most wordless converse; since dissolved
Into the sense with which love talks, my rest
Was troubled and yet sweet; my waking hours
Too full of care and pain.

ASIA:
Lift up thine eyes,                                              55
And let me read thy dream.

PANTHEA:
As I have said
With our sea-sister at his feet I slept.
The mountain mists, condensing at our voice
Under the moon, had spread their snowy flakes,
From the keen ice shielding our linked sleep.                    60
Then two dreams came. One, I remember not.
But in the other his pale wound-worn limbs
Fell from Prometheus, and the azure night
Grew radiant with the glory of that form
Which lives unchanged within, and his voice fell                 65
Like music which makes giddy the dim brain,
Faint with intoxication of keen joy:
'Sister of her whose footsteps pave the world
With loveliness—more fair than aught but her,
Whose shadow thou art—lift thine eyes on me.'                    70
I lifted them: the overpowering light
Of that immortal shape was shadowed o'er
By love; which, from his soft and flowing limbs,
And passion-parted lips, and keen, faint eyes,
Steamed forth like vaporous fire; an atmosphere                  75
Which wrapped me in its all-dissolving power,
As the warm ether of the morning sun
Wraps ere it drinks some cloud of wandering dew.
I saw not, heard not, moved not, only felt
His presence flow and mingle through my blood                    80
Till it became his life, and his grew mine,
And I was thus absorbed, until it passed,
And like the vapours when the sun sinks down,
Gathering again in drops upon the pines,
And tremulous as they, in the deep night                         85

My being was condensed; and as the rays
Of thought were slowly gathered, I could hear
His voice, whose accents lingered ere they died
Like footsteps of weak melody: thy name
Among the many sounds alone I heard                         90
Of what might be articulate; though still
I listened through the night when sound was none.
Ione wakened then, and said to me:
'Canst thou divine what troubles me to-night?
I always knew, what I desired before,                       95
Nor ever found delight to wish in vain.
But now I cannot tell thee what I seek;
I know not; something sweet, since it is sweet
Even to desire; it is thy sport, false sister;
Thou hast discovered some enchantment old,                  100
Whose spells have stolen my spirit as I slept
And mingled it with thine: for when just now
We kissed, I felt within thy parted lips
The sweet air that sustained me, and the warmth
Of the life-blood, for loss of which I faint,              105
Quivered between our intertwining arms.'
I answered not, for the Eastern star grew pale,
But fled to thee.

ASIA:
Thou speakest, but thy words
Are as the air: I feel them not: Oh, lift
Thine eyes, that I may read his written soul!              110

PANTHEA:
I lift them though they droop beneath the load
Of that they would express: what canst thou see
But thine own fairest shadow imaged there?

ASIA:
Thine eyes are like the deep, blue, boundless heaven
Contracted to two circles underneath                       115
Their long, fine lashes; dark, far, measureless,
Orb within orb, and line through line inwoven.

PANTHEA:
Why lookest thou as if a spirit passed?

ASIA:
There is a change: beyond their inmost depth
I see a shade, a shape: 'tis He, arrayed                          120
In the soft light of his own smiles, which spread
Like radiance from the cloud-surrounded moon.
Prometheus, it is thine! depart not yet!
Say not those smiles that we shall meet again
Within that bright pavilion which their beams              125
Shall build o'er the waste world? The dream is told.
What shape is that between us? Its rude hair
Roughens the wind that lifts it, its regard
Is wild and quick, yet 'tis a thing of air,
For through its gray robe gleams the golden dew          130
Whose stars the noon has quenched not.

DREAM
Follow! Follow!

PANTHEA:
It is mine other dream.

ASIA:
It disappears.

PANTHEA:
It passes now into my mind. Methought
As we sate here, the flower-infolding buds
Burst on yon lightning-blasted almond tree,                  135
When swift from the white Scythian wilderness
A wind swept forth wrinkling the Earth with frost:
I looked, and all the blossoms were blown down;
But on each leaf was stamped, as the blue bells
Of Hyacinth tell Apollo's written grief,                          140
O, FOLLOW, FOLLOW!

ASIA:
As you speak, your words
Fill, pause by pause, my own forgotten sleep
With shapes. Methought among these lawns together
We wandered, underneath the young gray dawn,
And multitudes of dense white fleecy clouds                145
Were wandering in thick flocks along the mountains

Shepherded by the slow, unwilling wind;
And the white dew on the new-bladed grass,
Just piercing the dark earth, hung silently;
And there was more which I remember not:                      150
But on the shadows of the morning clouds,
Athwart the purple mountain slope, was written
FOLLOW, O, FOLLOW! as they vanished by;
And on each herb, from which Heaven's dew had fallen,
The like was stamped, as with a withering fire;              155
A wind arose among the pines; it shook
The clinging music from their boughs, and then
Low, sweet, faint sounds, like the farewell of ghosts,
Were heard: O, FOLLOW, FOLLOW, FOLLOW ME!
And then I said, 'Panthea, look on me.'                       160
But in the depth of those beloved eyes
Still I saw, FOLLOW, FOLLOW!

ECHO:
Follow, follow!

PANTHEA:
The crags, this clear spring morning, mock our voices
As they were spirit-tongued.

ASIA:
It is some being
Around the crags. What fine clear sounds! O, list!           165

ECHOES, UNSEEN:
Echoes we: listen!
We cannot stay:
As dew-stars glisten
Then fade away—
Child of Ocean!                                               170

ASIA:
Hark! Spirits speak. The liquid responses
Of their aereal tongues yet sound.

PANTHEA:
I hear.

ECHOES:
Oh, follow, follow,
As our voice recedeth
Through the caverns hollow,                                    175
Where the forest spreadeth;
[MORE DISTANT.]
Oh, follow, follow!
Through the caverns hollow,
As the song floats thou pursue,
Where the wild bee never flew,                                 180
Through the noontide darkness deep,
By the odour-breathing sleep
Of faint night-flowers, and the waves
At the fountain-lighted caves,
While our music, wild and sweet,                               185
Mocks thy gently falling feet,
Child of Ocean!

ASIA:
Shall we pursue the sound? It grows more faint
And distant.

PANTHEA:
List! the strain floats nearer now.

ECHOES:
In the world unknown                                           190
Sleeps a voice unspoken;
By thy step alone
Can its rest be broken;
Child of Ocean!

ASIA:
How the notes sink upon the ebbing wind!                       195

ECHOES:
Oh, follow, follow!
Through the caverns hollow,
As the song floats thou pursue,
By the woodland noontide dew;
By the forests, lakes, and fountains,                          200
Through the many-folded mountains;

To the rents, and gulfs, and chasms,
Where the Earth reposed from spasms,
On the day when He and thou
Parted, to commingle now;                                       205
Child of Ocean!

ASIA:
Come, sweet Panthea, link thy hand in mine,
And follow, ere the voices fade away.

## SCENE 2.2: A FOREST, INTERMINGLED WITH ROCKS AND CAVERNS. ASIA AND PANTHEA PASS INTO IT. TWO YOUNG FAUNS ARE SITTING ON A ROCK LISTENING.

SEMICHORUS 1 OF SPIRITS:
The path through which that lovely twain
Have passed, by cedar, pine, and yew,
And each dark tree that ever grew,
Is curtained out from Heaven's wide blue;
Nor sun, nor moon, nor wind, nor rain,                          5
Can pierce its interwoven bowers,
Nor aught, save where some cloud of dew,
Drifted along the earth-creeping breeze,
Between the trunks of the hoar trees,
Hangs each a pearl in the pale flowers                          10
Of the green laurel, blown anew,
And bends, and then fades silently,
One frail and fair anemone:
Or when some star of many a one
That climbs and wanders through steep night,                    15
Has found the cleft through which alone
Beams fall from high those depths upon
Ere it is borne away, away,
By the swift Heavens that cannot stay,
It scatters drops of golden light,                              20
Like lines of rain that ne'er unite:
And the gloom divine is all around,
And underneath is the mossy ground.

SEMICHORUS 2:
There the voluptuous nightingales,
Are awake through all the broad noonday.                        25

When one with bliss or sadness fails,
And through the windless ivy-boughs,
Sick with sweet love, droops dying away
On its mate's music-panting bosom;
Another from the swinging blossom,                              30
Watching to catch the languid close
Of the last strain, then lifts on high
The wings of the weak melody,
Till some new strain of feeling bear
The song, and all the woods are mute;                           35
When there is heard through the dim air
The rush of wings, and rising there
Like many a lake-surrounded flute,
Sounds overflow the listener's brain
So sweet, that joy is almost pain.                              40

SEMICHORUS 1:
There those enchanted eddies play
Of echoes, music-tongued, which draw,
By Demogorgon's mighty law,
With melting rapture, or sweet awe,
All spirits on that secret way;                                 45
As inland boats are driven to Ocean
Down streams made strong with mountain-thaw:
And first there comes a gentle sound
To those in talk or slumber bound,
And wakes the destined soft emotion—                            50
Attracts, impels them; those who saw
Say from the breathing earth behind
There steams a plume-uplifting wind
Which drives them on their path, while they
Believe their own swift wings and feet                          55
The sweet desires within obey:
And so they float upon their way,
Until, still sweet, but loud and strong,
The storm of sound is driven along,
Sucked up and hurrying: as they fleet                           60
Behind, its gathering billows meet
And to the fatal mountain bear
Like clouds amid the yielding air.

FIRST FAUN:
Canst thou imagine where those spirits live
Which make such delicate music in the woods?                 65
We haunt within the least frequented caves
And closest coverts, and we know these wilds,
Yet never meet them, though we hear them oft:
Where may they hide themselves?

SECOND FAUN:
'Tis hard to tell;
I have heard those more skilled in spirits say,             70
The bubbles, which the enchantment of the sun
Sucks from the pale faint water-flowers that pave
The oozy bottom of clear lakes and pools,
Are the pavilions where such dwell and float
Under the green and golden atmosphere                       75
Which noontide kindles through the woven leaves;
And when these burst, and the thin fiery air,
The which they breathed within those lucent domes,
Ascends to flow like meteors through the night,
They ride on them, and rein their headlong speed,           80
And bow their burning crests, and glide in fire
Under the waters of the earth again.

FIRST FAUN:
If such live thus, have others other lives,
Under pink blossoms or within the bells
Of meadow flowers, or folded violets deep,                  85
Or on their dying odours, when they die,
Or in the sunlight of the sphered dew?

SECOND FAUN:
Ay, many more which we may well divine.
But should we stay to speak, noontide would come,
And thwart Silenus find his goats undrawn,                  90
And grudge to sing those wise and lovely songs
Of Fate, and Chance, and God, and Chaos old,
And Love, and the chained Titan's woeful doom,
And how he shall be loosed, and make the earth
One brotherhood: delightful strains which cheer            95
Our solitary twilights, and which charm
To silence the unenvying nightingales.

## SCENE 2.3: A PINNACLE OF ROCK AMONG MOUNTAINS.
## ASIA AND PANTHEA.

PANTHEA:
Hither the sound has borne us—to the realm
Of Demogorgon, and the mighty portal,
Like a volcano's meteor-breathing chasm,
Whence the oracular vapour is hurled up
Which lonely men drink wandering in their youth,          5
And call truth, virtue, love, genius, or joy,
That maddening wine of life, whose dregs they drain
To deep intoxication; and uplift,
Like Maenads who cry loud, Evoe! Evoe!
The voice which is contagion to the world.               10

ASIA:
Fit throne for such a Power! Magnificent!
How glorious art thou, Earth! And if thou be
The shadow of some spirit lovelier still,
Though evil stain its work, and it should be
Like its creation, weak yet beautiful,                   15
I could fall down and worship that and thee.
Even now my heart adoreth: Wonderful!
Look, sister, ere the vapour dim thy brain:
Beneath is a wide plain of billowy mist,
As a lake, paving in the morning sky,                    20
With azure waves which burst in silver light,
Some Indian vale. Behold it, rolling on
Under the curdling winds, and islanding
The peak whereon we stand, midway, around,
Encinctured by the dark and blooming forests,            25
Dim twilight-lawns, and stream-illumined caves,
And wind-enchanted shapes of wandering mist;
And far on high the keen sky-cleaving mountains
From icy spires of sun-like radiance fling
The dawn, as lifted Ocean's dazzling spray,              30
From some Atlantic islet scattered up,
Spangles the wind with lamp-like water-drops.
The vale is girdled with their walls, a howl
Of cataracts from their thaw-cloven ravines,
Satiates the listening wind, continuous, vast,           35
Awful as silence. Hark! the rushing snow!

The sun-awakened avalanche! whose mass,
Thrice sifted by the storm, had gathered there
Flake after flake, in heaven-defying minds
As thought by thought is piled, till some great truth                    40
Is loosened, and the nations echo round,
Shaken to their roots, as do the mountains now.

PANTHEA:
Look how the gusty sea of mist is breaking
In crimson foam, even at our feet! it rises
As Ocean at the enchantment of the moon                                   45
Round foodless men wrecked on some oozy isle.

ASIA:
The fragments of the cloud are scattered up;
The wind that lifts them disentwines my hair;
Its billows now sweep o'er mine eyes; my brain
Grows dizzy; see'st thou shapes within the mist?                          50

PANTHEA:
A countenance with beckoning smiles: there burns
An azure fire within its golden locks!
Another and another: hark! they speak!

SONG OF SPIRITS:
To the deep, to the deep,
Down, down!                                                               55
Through the shade of sleep,
Through the cloudy strife
Of Death and of Life;
Through the veil and the bar
Of things which seem and are                                              60
Even to the steps of the remotest throne,
Down, down!

While the sound whirls around,
Down, down!
As the fawn draws the hound,                                              65
As the lightning the vapour,
As a weak moth the taper;
Death, despair; love, sorrow;
Time both; to-day, to-morrow;

As steel obeys the spirit of the stone,                              70
Down, down!

Through the gray, void abysm,
Down, down!
Where the air is no prism,
And the moon and stars are not,                                      75
And the cavern-crags wear not
The radiance of Heaven,
Nor the gloom to Earth given,
Where there is One pervading, One alone,
Down, down!                                                          80

In the depth of the deep,
Down, down!
Like veiled lightning asleep,
Like the spark nursed in embers,
The last look Love remembers,                                        85
Like a diamond, which shines
On the dark wealth of mines,
A spell is treasured but for thee alone.
Down, down!

We have bound thee, we guide thee;                                   90
Down, down!
With the bright form beside thee;
Resist not the weakness,
Such strength is in meekness
That the Eternal, the Immortal,                                      95
Must unloose through life's portal
The snake-like Doom coiled underneath his throne
By that alone.

## SCENE 2.4: THE CAVE OF DEMOGORGON.
## ASIA AND PANTHEA.

PANTHEA:
What veiled form sits on that ebon throne?

ASIA:
The veil has fallen.

PANTHEA:
I see a mighty darkness
Filling the seat of power, and rays of gloom
Dart round, as light from the meridian sun.
—Ungazed upon and shapeless; neither limb,                    5
Nor form, nor outline; yet we feel it is
A living Spirit.

DEMOGORGON:
Ask what thou wouldst know.

ASIA:
What canst thou tell?

DEMOGORGON:
All things thou dar'st demand.

ASIA:
Who made the living world?

DEMOGORGON:
God.

ASIA:
Who made all
That it contains? thought, passion, reason, will,              10
Imagination?

DEMOGORGON:
God: Almighty God.

ASIA:
Who made that sense which, when the winds of Spring
In rarest visitation, or the voice
Of one beloved heard in youth alone,
Fills the faint eyes with falling tears which dim              15
The radiant looks of unbewailing flowers,
And leaves this peopled earth a solitude
When it returns no more?

DEMOGORGON:
Merciful God.

ASIA:
And who made terror, madness, crime, remorse,
Which from the links of the great chain of things,                    20
To every thought within the mind of man
Sway and drag heavily, and each one reels
Under the load towards the pit of death;
Abandoned hope, and love that turns to hate;
And self-contempt, bitterer to drink than blood;                      25
Pain, whose unheeded and familiar speech
Is howling, and keen shrieks, day after day;
And Hell, or the sharp fear of Hell?

DEMOGORGON:
He reigns.

ASIA:
Utter his name: a world pining in pain
Asks but his name: curses shall drag him down.                        30

DEMOGORGON:
He reigns.

ASIA:
I feel, I know it: who?

DEMOGORGON:
He reigns.

ASIA:
Who reigns? There was the Heaven and Earth at first,
And Light and Love; then Saturn, from whose throne
Time fell, an envious shadow: such the state
Of the earth's primal spirits beneath his sway,                       35
As the calm joy of flowers and living leaves
Before the wind or sun has withered them
And semivital worms; but he refused
The birthright of their being, knowledge, power,
The skill which wields the elements, the thought                      40
Which pierces this dim universe like light,
Self-empire, and the majesty of love;
For thirst of which they fainted. Then Prometheus
Gave wisdom, which is strength, to Jupiter,

And with this law alone, 'Let man be free,'                    45
Clothed him with the dominion of wide Heaven.
To know nor faith, nor love, nor law; to be
Omnipotent but friendless is to reign;
And Jove now reigned; for on the race of man
First famine, and then toil, and then disease,                 50
Strife, wounds, and ghastly death unseen before,
Fell; and the unseasonable seasons drove
With alternating shafts of frost and fire,
Their shelterless, pale tribes to mountain caves:
And in their desert hearts fierce wants he sent,              55
And mad disquietudes, and shadows idle
Of unreal good, which levied mutual war,
So ruining the lair wherein they raged.
Prometheus saw, and waked the legioned hopes
Which sleep within folded Elysian flowers,                    60
Nepenthe, Moly, Amaranth, fadeless blooms,
That they might hide with thin and rainbow wings
The shape of Death; and Love he sent to bind
The disunited tendrils of that vine
Which bears the wine of life, the human heart;                65
And he tamed fire which, like some beast of prey,
Most terrible, but lovely, played beneath
The frown of man; and tortured to his will
Iron and gold, the slaves and signs of power,
And gems and poisons, and all subtlest forms                  70
Hidden beneath the mountains and the waves.
He gave man speech, and speech created thought,
Which is the measure of the universe;
And Science struck the thrones of earth and heaven,
Which shook, but fell not; and the harmonious mind            75
Poured itself forth in all-prophetic song;
And music lifted up the listening spirit
Until it walked, exempt from mortal care,
Godlike, o'er the clear billows of sweet sound;
And human hands first mimicked and then mocked,               80
With moulded limbs more lovely than its own,
The human form, till marble grew divine;
And mothers, gazing, drank the love men see
Reflected in their race, behold, and perish.
He told the hidden power of herbs and springs,                85
And Disease drank and slept. Death grew like sleep.

He taught the implicated orbits woven
Of the wide-wandering stars; and how the sun
Changes his lair, and by what secret spell
The pale moon is transformed, when her broad eye                    90
Gazes not on the interlunar sea:
He taught to rule, as life directs the limbs,
The tempest-winged chariots of the Ocean,
And the Celt knew the Indian. Cities then
Were built, and through their snow-like columns flowed              95
The warm winds, and the azure ether shone,
And the blue sea and shadowy hills were seen.
Such, the alleviations of his state,
Prometheus gave to man, for which he hangs
Withering in destined pain: but who rains down                     100
Evil, the immedicable plague, which, while
Man looks on his creation like a God
And sees that it is glorious, drives him on,
The wreck of his own will, the scorn of earth,
The outcast, the abandoned, the alone?                             105
Not Jove: while yet his frown shook Heaven ay, when
His adversary from adamantine chains
Cursed him, he trembled like a slave. Declare
Who is his master? Is he too a slave?

DEMOGORGON:
All spirits are enslaved which serve things evil:                  110
Thou knowest if Jupiter be such or no.

ASIA:
Whom calledst thou God?

DEMOGORGON:
I spoke but as ye speak,
For Jove is the supreme of living things.

ASIA:
Who is the master of the slave?

DEMOGORGON:
If the abysm
Could vomit forth its secrets...But a voice                        115
Is wanting, the deep truth is imageless;

For what would it avail to bid thee gaze
On the revolving world? What to bid speak
Fate, Time, Occasion, Chance and Change? To these
All things are subject but eternal Love.                          120

ASIA:
So much I asked before, and my heart gave
The response thou hast given; and of such truths
Each to itself must be the oracle.
One more demand; and do thou answer me
As my own soul would answer, did it know                          125
That which I ask. Prometheus shall arise
Henceforth the sun of this rejoicing world:
When shall the destined hour arrive?

DEMOGORGON:
Behold!

ASIA:
The rocks are cloven, and through the purple night
I see cars drawn by rainbow-winged steeds                         130
Which trample the dim winds: in each there stands
A wild-eyed charioteer urging their flight.
Some look behind, as fiends pursued them there,
And yet I see no shapes but the keen stars:
Others, with burning eyes, lean forth, and drink                  135
With eager lips the wind of their own speed,
As if the thing they loved fled on before,
And now, even now, they clasped it. Their bright locks
Stream like a comet's flashing hair; they all
Sweep onward.

DEMOGORGON:
These are the immortal Hours,                                     140
Of whom thou didst demand. One waits for thee.

ASIA:
A Spirit with a dreadful countenance
Checks its dark chariot by the craggy gulf.
Unlike thy brethren, ghastly charioteer,
Who art thou? Whither wouldst thou bear me? Speak!                145

SPIRIT:
I am the shadow of a destiny
More dread than is my aspect: ere yon planet
Has set, the darkness which ascends with me
Shall wrap in lasting night heaven's kingless throne.

ASIA:
What meanest thou?

PANTHEA:
That terrible shadow floats                                    150
Up from its throne, as may the lurid smoke
Of earthquake-ruined cities o'er the sea.
Lo! it ascends the car; the coursers fly
Terrified: watch its path among the stars
Blackening the night!

ASIA:
Thus I am answered: strange!                                   155

PANTHEA:
See, near the verge, another chariot stays;
An ivory shell inlaid with crimson fire,
Which comes and goes within its sculptured rim
Of delicate strange tracery; the young spirit
That guides it has the dove-like eyes of hope;               160
How its soft smiles attract the soul! as light
Lures winged insects through the lampless air.

SPIRIT:
My coursers are fed with the lightning,
They drink of the whirlwind's stream,
And when the red morning is bright'ning                       165
They bathe in the fresh sunbeam;
They have strength for their swiftness I deem;
Then ascend with me, daughter of Ocean.
I desire: and their speed makes night kindle;
I fear: they outstrip the Typhoon;                            170
Ere the cloud piled on Atlas can dwindle
We encircle the earth and the moon:
We shall rest from long labours at noon:
Then ascend with me, daughter of Ocean.

## SCENE 2.5: THE CAR PAUSES WITHIN A CLOUD ON THE TOP OF A SNOWY MOUNTAIN. ASIA, PANTHEA, AND THE SPIRIT OF THE HOUR.

SPIRIT:
On the brink of the night and the morning
My coursers are wont to respire;
But the Earth has just whispered a warning
That their flight must be swifter than fire:
They shall drink the hot speed of desire!                        5

ASIA:
Thou breathest on their nostrils, but my breath
Would give them swifter speed.

SPIRIT:
Alas! it could not.

PANTHEA:
Oh Spirit! pause, and tell whence is the light
Which fills this cloud? the sun is yet unrisen.

SPIRIT:
The sun will rise not until noon. Apollo                          10
Is held in heaven by wonder; and the light
Which fills this vapour, as the aereal hue
Of fountain-gazing roses fills the water,
Flows from thy mighty sister.

PANTHEA:
Yes, I feel—

ASIA:
What is it with thee, sister? Thou art pale.                      15

PANTHEA:
How thou art changed! I dare not look on thee;
I feel but see thee not. I scarce endure
The radiance of thy beauty. Some good change
Is working in the elements, which suffer
Thy presence thus unveiled. The Nereids tell                      20
That on the day when the clear hyaline

Was cloven at thine uprise, and thou didst stand
Within a veined shell, which floated on
Over the calm floor of the crystal sea,
Among the Aegean isles, and by the shores                    25
Which bear thy name; love, like the atmosphere
Of the sun's fire filling the living world,
Burst from thee, and illumined earth and heaven
And the deep ocean and the sunless caves
And all that dwells within them; till grief cast            30
Eclipse upon the soul from which it came:
Such art thou now; nor is it I alone,
Thy sister, thy companion, thine own chosen one,
But the whole world which seeks thy sympathy.
Hearest thou not sounds i' the air which speak the love     35
Of all articulate beings? Feelest thou not
The inanimate winds enamoured of thee? List!

[MUSIC.]

ASIA:
Thy words are sweeter than aught else but his
Whose echoes they are; yet all love is sweet,
Given or returned. Common as light is love,                 40
And its familiar voice wearies not ever.
Like the wide heaven, the all-sustaining air,
It makes the reptile equal to the God:
They who inspire it most are fortunate,
As I am now; but those who feel it most                     45
Are happier still, after long sufferings,
As I shall soon become.

PANTHEA:
List! Spirits speak.

VOICE IN THE AIR, SINGING:
Life of Life! thy lips enkindle
With their love the breath between them;
And thy smiles before they dwindle                          50
Make the cold air fire; then screen them
In those looks, where whoso gazes
Faints, entangled in their mazes.

Child of Light! thy limbs are burning
Through the vest which seems to hide them;                    55
As the radiant lines of morning
Through the clouds ere they divide them;
And this atmosphere divinest
Shrouds thee wheresoe'er thou shinest.

Fair are others; none beholds thee,                           60
But thy voice sounds low and tender
Like the fairest, for it folds thee
From the sight, that liquid splendour,
And all feel, yet see thee never,
As I feel now, lost for ever!                                 65

Lamp of Earth! where'er thou movest
Its dim shapes are clad with brightness,
And the souls of whom thou lovest
Walk upon the winds with lightness,
Till they fail, as I am failing,                              70
Dizzy, lost, yet unbewailing!

ASIA:
My soul is an enchanted boat,
Which, like a sleeping swan, doth float
Upon the silver waves of thy sweet singing;
And thine doth like an angel sit                              75
Beside a helm conducting it,
Whilst all the winds with melody are ringing.
It seems to float ever, for ever,
Upon that many-winding river,
Between mountains, woods, abysses,                            80
A paradise of wildernesses!
Till, like one in slumber bound,
Borne to the ocean, I float down, around,
Into a sea profound, of ever-spreading sound:

Meanwhile thy spirit lifts its pinions                        85
In music's most serene dominions;
Catching the winds that fan that happy heaven.
And we sail on, away, afar,
Without a course, without a star,
But, by the instinct of sweet music driven;                  90

Till through Elysian garden islets
By thee most beautiful of pilots,
Where never mortal pinnace glided,
The boat of my desire is guided:
Realms where the air we breathe is love,                    95
Which in the winds and on the waves doth move,
Harmonizing this earth with what we feel above.

We have passed Age's icy caves,
And Manhood's dark and tossing waves,
And Youth's smooth ocean, smiling to betray:               100
Beyond the glassy gulfs we flee
Of shadow-peopled Infancy,
Through Death and Birth, to a diviner day;
A paradise of vaulted bowers,
Lit by downward-gazing flowers,                            105
And watery paths that wind between
Wildernesses calm and green,
Peopled by shapes too bright to see,
And rest, having beheld; somewhat like thee;
Which walk upon the sea, and chant melodiously!           110

## ACT 3.

### SCENE 3.1: HEAVEN. JUPITER ON HIS THRONE; THETIS AND THE OTHER DEITIES ASSEMBLED.

JUPITER:
Ye congregated powers of heaven, who share
The glory and the strength of him ye serve,
Rejoice! henceforth I am omnipotent.
All else had been subdued to me; alone
The soul of man, like unextinguished fire,                   5
Yet burns towards heaven with fierce reproach, and doubt,
And lamentation, and reluctant prayer,
Hurling up insurrection, which might make
Our antique empire insecure, though built
On eldest faith, and hell's coeval, fear;                   10
And though my curses through the pendulous air,
Like snow on herbless peaks, fall flake by flake,
And cling to it; though under my wrath's night

It climbs the crags of life, step after step,
Which wound it, as ice wounds unsandalled feet,               15
It yet remains supreme o'er misery,
Aspiring, unrepressed, yet soon to fall:
Even now have I begotten a strange wonder,
That fatal child, the terror of the earth,
Who waits but till the destined hour arrive,                  20
Bearing from Demogorgon's vacant throne
The dreadful might of ever-living limbs
Which clothed that awful spirit unbeheld,
To redescend, and trample out the spark.
Pour forth heaven's wine, Idaean Ganymede,                    25
And let it fill the Daedal cups like fire,
And from the flower-inwoven soil divine
Ye all-triumphant harmonies arise,
As dew from earth under the twilight stars:
Drink! be the nectar circling through your veins              30
The soul of joy, ye ever-living Gods,
Till exultation burst in one wide voice
Like music from Elysian winds.
And thou
Ascend beside me, veiled in the light
Of the desire which makes thee one with me,                   35
Thetis, bright image of eternity!
When thou didst cry, 'Insufferable might!
God! Spare me! I sustain not the quick flames,
The penetrating presence; all my being,
Like him whom the Numidian seps did thaw                      40
Into a dew with poison, is dissolved,
Sinking through its foundations—even then
Two mighty spirits, mingling, made a third
Mightier than either, which, unbodied now,
Between us floats, felt, although unbeheld,                   45
Waiting the incarnation, which ascends,
(Hear ye the thunder of the fiery wheels
Griding the winds?) from Demogorgon's throne.
Victory! victory! Feel'st thou not, O world,
The earthquake of his chariot thundering up                   50
Olympus?
[THE CAR OF THE HOUR ARRIVES. DEMOGORGON DESCENDS,
AND MOVES TOWARDS THE THRONE OF JUPITER.]
Awful shape, what art thou? Speak!

DEMOGORGON:
Eternity. Demand no direr name.
Descend, and follow me down the abyss.
I am thy child, as thou wert Saturn's child;
Mightier than thee: and we must dwell together                55
Henceforth in darkness. Lift thy lightnings not.
The tyranny of heaven none may retain,
Or reassume, or hold, succeeding thee:
Yet if thou wilt, as 'tis the destiny
Of trodden worms to writhe till they are dead,                60
Put forth thy might.

JUPITER:
Detested prodigy!
Even thus beneath the deep Titanian prisons
I trample thee! thou lingerest?
Mercy! mercy!
No pity, no release, no respite! Oh,
That thou wouldst make mine enemy my judge,                   65
Even where he hangs, seared by my long revenge,
On Caucasus! he would not doom me thus.
Gentle, and just, and dreadless, is he not
The monarch of the world? What then art thou?
No refuge! no appeal!
Sink with me then,                                            70
We two will sink on the wide waves of ruin,
Even as a vulture and a snake outspent
Drop, twisted in inextricable fight,
Into a shoreless sea. Let hell unlock
Its mounded oceans of tempestuous fire,                       75
And whelm on them into the bottomless void
This desolated world, and thee, and me,
The conqueror and the conquered, and the wreck
Of that for which they combated.
Ai, Ai!
The elements obey me not. I sink                              80
Dizzily down, ever, for ever, down.
And, like a cloud, mine enemy above
Darkens my fall with victory! Ai, Ai!

## SCENE 3.2: THE MOUTH OF A GREAT RIVER IN THE ISLAND ATLANTIS. OCEAN IS DISCOVERED RECLINING NEAR THE SHORE; APOLLO STANDS BESIDE HIM.

OCEAN:
He fell, thou sayest, beneath his conqueror's frown?

APOLLO:
Ay, when the strife was ended which made dim
The orb I rule, and shook the solid stars,
The terrors of his eye illumined heaven
With sanguine light, through the thick ragged skirts          5
Of the victorious darkness, as he fell:
Like the last glare of day's red agony,
Which, from a rent among the fiery clouds,
Burns far along the tempest-wrinkled deep.

OCEAN:
He sunk to the abyss? To the dark void?                       10

APOLLO:
An eagle so caught in some bursting cloud
On Caucasus, his thunder-baffled wings
Entangled in the whirlwind, and his eyes
Which gazed on the undazzling sun, now blinded
By the white lightning, while the ponderous hail             15
Beats on his struggling form, which sinks at length
Prone, and the aereal ice clings over it.

OCEAN:
Henceforth the fields of heaven-reflecting sea
Which are my realm, will heave, unstained with blood,
Beneath the uplifting winds, like plains of corn             20
Swayed by the summer air; my streams will flow
Round many-peopled continents, and round
Fortunate isles; and from their glassy thrones
Blue Proteus and his humid nymphs shall mark
The shadow of fair ships, as mortals see                     25
The floating bark of the light-laden moon
With that white star, its sightless pilot's crest,
Borne down the rapid sunset's ebbing sea;
Tracking their path no more by blood and groans,

And desolation, and the mingled voice                                30
Of slavery and command; but by the light
Of wave-reflected flowers, and floating odours,
And music soft, and mild, free, gentle voices,
And sweetest music, such as spirits love.

APOLLO:
And I shall gaze not on the deeds which make                         35
My mind obscure with sorrow, as eclipse
Darkens the sphere I guide; but list, I hear
The small, clear, silver lute of the young Spirit
That sits i' the morning star.

OCEAN:
Thou must away;
Thy steeds will pause at even, till when farewell:                   40
The loud deep calls me home even now to feed it
With azure calm out of the emerald urns
Which stand for ever full beside my throne.
Behold the Nereids under the green sea,
Their wavering limbs borne on the wind-like stream,                  45
Their white arms lifted o'er their streaming hair
With garlands pied and starry sea-flower crowns,
Hastening to grace their mighty sister's joy.
[A SOUND OF WAVES IS HEARD.]
It is the unpastured sea hungering for calm.
Peace, monster; I come now. Farewell.

APOLLO:
Farewell.                                                            50

## SCENE 3.3: CAUCASUS. PROMETHEUS, HERCULES, IONE, THE EARTH, SPIRITS, ASIA, AND PANTHEA, BORNE IN THE CAR WITH THE SPIRIT OF THE HOUR. HERCULES UNBINDS PROMETHEUS, WHO DESCENDS.

HERCULES:
Most glorious among Spirits, thus doth strength
To wisdom, courage, and long-suffering love,
And thee, who art the form they animate,
Minister like a slave.

PROMETHEUS:
Thy gentle words
Are sweeter even than freedom long desired                    5
And long delayed.
Asia, thou light of life,
Shadow of beauty unbeheld: and ye,
Fair sister nymphs, who made long years of pain
Sweet to remember, through your love and care:
Henceforth we will not part. There is a cave,                10
All overgrown with trailing odorous plants,
Which curtain out the day with leaves and flowers,
And paved with veined emerald, and a fountain
Leaps in the midst with an awakening sound.
From its curved roof the mountain's frozen tears             15
Like snow, or silver, or long diamond spires,
Hang downward, raining forth a doubtful light:
And there is heard the ever-moving air,
Whispering without from tree to tree, and birds,
And bees; and all around are mossy seats,                    20
And the rough walls are clothed with long soft grass;
A simple dwelling, which shall be our own;
Where we will sit and talk of time and change,
As the world ebbs and flows, ourselves unchanged.
What can hide man from mutability?                           25
And if ye sigh, then I will smile; and thou,
Ione, shalt chant fragments of sea-music,
Until I weep, when ye shall smile away
The tears she brought, which yet were sweet to shed.
We will entangle buds and flowers and beams                  30
Which twinkle on the fountain's brim, and make
Strange combinations out of common things,
Like human babes in their brief innocence;
And we will search, with looks and words of love,
For hidden thoughts, each lovelier than the last,            35
Our unexhausted spirits; and like lutes
Touched by the skill of the enamoured wind,
Weave harmonies divine, yet ever new,
From difference sweet where discord cannot be;
And hither come, sped on the charmed winds,                  40
Which meet from all the points of heaven, as bees
From every flower aereal Enna feeds,
At their known island-homes in Himera,

The echoes of the human world, which tell
Of the low voice of love, almost unheard,                          45
And dove-eyed pity's murmured pain, and music,
Itself the echo of the heart, and all
That tempers or improves man's life, now free;
And lovely apparitions—dim at first,
Then radiant, as the mind, arising bright                          50
From the embrace of beauty (whence the forms
Of which these are the phantoms) casts on them
The gathered rays which are reality—
Shall visit us, the progeny immortal
Of Painting, Sculpture, and rapt Poesy,                          55
And arts, though unimagined, yet to be.
The wandering voices and the shadows these
Of all that man becomes, the mediators
Of that best worship love, by him and us
Given and returned; swift shapes and sounds, which grow          60
More fair and soft as man grows wise and kind,
And, veil by veil, evil and error fall:
Such virtue has the cave and place around.
[TURNING TO THE SPIRIT OF THE HOUR.]
For thee, fair Spirit, one toil remains. Ione,
Give her that curved shell, which Proteus old                          65
Made Asia's nuptial boon, breathing within it
A voice to be accomplished, and which thou
Didst hide in grass under the hollow rock.

IONE:
Thou most desired Hour, more loved and lovely
Than all thy sisters, this is the mystic shell;                          70
See the pale azure fading into silver
Lining it with a soft yet glowing light:
Looks it not like lulled music sleeping there?

SPIRIT:
It seems in truth the fairest shell of Ocean:
Its sound must be at once both sweet and strange.                          75

PROMETHEUS:
Go, borne over the cities of mankind
On whirlwind-footed coursers: once again
Outspeed the sun around the orbed world;

And as thy chariot cleaves the kindling air,
Thou breathe into the many-folded shell,                              80
Loosening its mighty music; it shall be
As thunder mingled with clear echoes: then
Return; and thou shalt dwell beside our cave.
And thou, O Mother Earth!—

THE EARTH:
I hear, I feel;
Thy lips are on me, and thy touch runs down                           85
Even to the adamantine central gloom
Along these marble nerves; 'tis life, 'tis joy,
And, through my withered, old, and icy frame
The warmth of an immortal youth shoots down
Circling. Henceforth the many children fair                           90
Folded in my sustaining arms; all plants,
And creeping forms, and insects rainbow-winged,
And birds, and beasts, and fish, and human shapes,
Which drew disease and pain from my wan bosom,
Draining the poison of despair, shall take                            95
And interchange sweet nutriment; to me
Shall they become like sister-antelopes
By one fair dam, snow-white and swift as wind,
Nursed among lilies near a brimming stream.
The dew-mists of my sunless sleep shall float                        100
Under the stars like balm: night-folded flowers
Shall suck unwithering hues in their repose:
And men and beasts in happy dreams shall gather
Strength for the coming day, and all its joy:
And death shall be the last embrace of her                           105
Who takes the life she gave, even as a mother,
Folding her child, says, 'Leave me not again.'

ASIA:
Oh, mother! wherefore speak the name of death?
Cease they to love, and move, and breathe, and speak,
Who die?

THE EARTH:
It would avail not to reply:                                          110
Thou art immortal, and this tongue is known
But to the uncommunicating dead.

Death is the veil which those who live call life:
They sleep, and it is lifted: and meanwhile
In mild variety the seasons mild　　　　　　　　　　115
With rainbow-skirted showers, and odorous winds,
And long blue meteors cleansing the dull night,
And the life-kindling shafts of the keen sun's
All-piercing bow, and the dew-mingled rain
Of the calm moonbeams, a soft influence mild,　　120
Shall clothe the forests and the fields, ay, even
The crag-built deserts of the barren deep,
With ever-living leaves, and fruits, and flowers.
And thou! There is a cavern where my spirit
Was panted forth in anguish whilst thy pain　　　125
Made my heart mad, and those who did inhale it
Became mad too, and built a temple there,
And spoke, and were oracular, and lured
The erring nations round to mutual war,
And faithless faith, such as Jove kept with thee;　130
Which breath now rises, as amongst tall weeds
A violet's exhalation, and it fills
With a serener light and crimson air
Intense, yet soft, the rocks and woods around;
It feeds the quick growth of the serpent vine,　　135
And the dark linked ivy tangling wild,
And budding, blown, or odour-faded blooms
Which star the winds with points of coloured light,
As they rain through them, and bright golden globes
Of fruit, suspended in their own green heaven,　　140
And through their veined leaves and amber stems
The flowers whose purple and translucid bowls
Stand ever mantling with aereal dew,
The drink of spirits: and it circles round,
Like the soft waving wings of noonday dreams,　　145
Inspiring calm and happy thoughts, like mine,
Now thou art thus restored. This cave is thine.
Arise! Appear!
[A SPIRIT RISES IN THE LIKENESS OF A WINGED CHILD.]
This is my torch-bearer;
Who let his lamp out in old time with gazing
On eyes from which he kindled it anew　　　　　150
With love, which is as fire, sweet daughter mine,
For such is that within thine own. Run, wayward,

And guide this company beyond the peak
Of Bacchic Nysa, Maenad-haunted mountain,
And beyond Indus and its tribute rivers,                    155
Trampling the torrent streams and glassy lakes
With feet unwet, unwearied, undelaying,
And up the green ravine, across the vale,
Beside the windless and crystalline pool,
Where ever lies, on unerasing waves,                        160
The image of a temple, built above,
Distinct with column, arch, and architrave,
And palm-like capital, and over-wrought,
And populous with most living imagery,
Praxitelean shapes, whose marble smiles                     165
Fill the hushed air with everlasting love.
It is deserted now, but once it bore
Thy name, Prometheus; there the emulous youths
Bore to thy honour through the divine gloom
The lamp which was thine emblem; even as those              170
Who bear the untransmitted torch of hope
Into the grave, across the night of life,
As thou hast borne it most triumphantly
To this far goal of Time. Depart, farewell.
Beside that temple is the destined cave.                    175

## SCENE 3.4: A FOREST. IN THE BACKGROUND A CAVE. PROMETHEUS, ASIA, PANTHEA, IONE, AND THE SPIRIT OF THE EARTH.

IONE:
Sister, it is not earthly: how it glides
Under the leaves! how on its head there burns
A light, like a green star, whose emerald beams
Are twined with its fair hair! how, as it moves,
The splendour drops in flakes upon the grass!               5
Knowest thou it?

PANTHEA:
It is the delicate spirit
That guides the earth through heaven. From afar
The populous constellations call that light
The loveliest of the planets; and sometimes
It floats along the spray of the salt sea,                  10

Or makes its chariot of a foggy cloud,
Or walks through fields or cities while men sleep,
Or o'er the mountain tops, or down the rivers,
Or through the green waste wilderness, as now,
Wondering at all it sees. Before Jove reigned                    15
It loved our sister Asia, and it came
Each leisure hour to drink the liquid light
Out of her eyes, for which it said it thirsted
As one bit by a dipsas, and with her
It made its childish confidence, and told her            20
All it had known or seen, for it saw much,
Yet idly reasoned what it saw; and called her—
For whence it sprung it knew not, nor do I—
Mother, dear mother.

THE SPIRIT OF THE EARTH [RUNNING TO ASIA]:
Mother, dearest mother;
May I then talk with thee as I was wont?                    25
May I then hide my eyes in thy soft arms,
After thy looks have made them tired of joy?
May I then play beside thee the long noons,
When work is none in the bright silent air?

ASIA:
I love thee, gentlest being, and henceforth                  30
Can cherish thee unenvied: speak, I pray:
Thy simple talk once solaced, now delights.

SPIRIT OF THE EARTH:
Mother, I am grown wiser, though a child
Cannot be wise like thee, within this day;
And happier too; happier and wiser both.                    35
Thou knowest that toads, and snakes, and loathly worms,
And venomous and malicious beasts, and boughs
That bore ill berries in the woods, were ever
An hindrance to my walks o'er the green world:
And that, among the haunts of humankind,                    40
Hard-featured men, or with proud, angry looks,
Or cold, staid gait, or false and hollow smiles,
Or the dull sneer of self-loved ignorance,
Or other such foul masks, with which ill thoughts
Hide that fair being whom we spirits call man;          45

And women too, ugliest of all things evil,
(Though fair, even in a world where thou art fair,
When good and kind, free and sincere like thee)
When false or frowning made me sick at heart
To pass them, though they slept, and I unseen.                    50
Well, my path lately lay through a great city
Into the woody hills surrounding it:
A sentinel was sleeping at the gate:
When there was heard a sound, so loud, it shook
The towers amid the moonlight, yet more sweet                     55
Than any voice but thine, sweetest of all;
A long, long sound, as it would never end:
And all the inhabitants leaped suddenly
Out of their rest, and gathered in the streets,
Looking in wonder up to Heaven, while yet                         60
The music pealed along. I hid myself
Within a fountain in the public square,
Where I lay like the reflex of the moon
Seen in a wave under green leaves; and soon
Those ugly human shapes and visages                              65
Of which I spoke as having wrought me pain,
Passed floating through the air, and fading still
Into the winds that scattered them; and those
From whom they passed seemed mild and lovely forms
After some foul disguise had fallen, and all                     70
Were somewhat changed, and after brief surprise
And greetings of delighted wonder, all
Went to their sleep again: and when the dawn
Came, wouldst thou think that toads, and snakes, and efts,
Could e'er be beautiful? yet so they were,                       75
And that with little change of shape or hue:
All things had put their evil nature off:
I cannot tell my joy, when o'er a lake,
Upon a drooping bough with nightshade twined,
I saw two azure halcyons clinging downward                       80
And thinning one bright bunch of amber berries,
With quick long beaks, and in the deep there lay
Those lovely forms imaged as in a sky;
So, with my thoughts full of these happy changes,
We meet again, the happiest change of all.                       85

ASIA:
And never will we part, till thy chaste sister
Who guides the frozen and inconstant moon
Will look on thy more warm and equal light
Till her heart thaw like flakes of April snow
And love thee.

SPIRIT OF THE EARTH:
What! as Asia loves Prometheus? 90

ASIA:
Peace, wanton, thou art yet not old enough.
Think ye by gazing on each other's eyes
To multiply your lovely selves, and fill
With sphered fires the interlunar air?

SPIRIT OF THE EARTH:
Nay, mother, while my sister trims her lamp
'Tis hard I should go darkling. 95

ASIA:
Listen; look!

[THE SPIRIT OF THE HOUR ENTERS.]

PROMETHEUS:
We feel what thou hast heard and seen: yet speak.

SPIRIT OF THE HOUR:
Soon as the sound had ceased whose thunder filled
The abysses of the sky and the wide earth,
There was a change: the impalpable thin air 100
And the all-circling sunlight were transformed,
As if the sense of love dissolved in them
Had folded itself round the sphered world.
My vision then grew clear, and I could see
Into the mysteries of the universe: 105
Dizzy as with delight I floated down,
Winnowing the lightsome air with languid plumes,
My coursers sought their birthplace in the sun,
Where they henceforth will live exempt from toil,
Pasturing flowers of vegetable fire; 110

And where my moonlike car will stand within
A temple, gazed upon by Phidian forms
Of thee, and Asia, and the Earth, and me,
And you fair nymphs looking the love we feel—
In memory of the tidings it has borne—                              115
Beneath a dome fretted with graven flowers,
Poised on twelve columns of resplendent stone,
And open to the bright and liquid sky.
Yoked to it by an amphisbaenic snake
The likeness of those winged steeds will mock                       120
The flight from which they find repose. Alas,
Whither has wandered now my partial tongue
When all remains untold which ye would hear?
As I have said, I floated to the earth:
It was, as it is still, the pain of bliss                           125
To move, to breathe, to be. I wandering went
Among the haunts and dwellings of mankind,
And first was disappointed not to see
Such mighty change as I had felt within
Expressed in outward things; but soon I looked,                     130
And behold, thrones were kingless, and men walked
One with the other even as spirits do,
None fawned, none trampled; hate, disdain, or fear,
Self-love or self-contempt, on human brows
No more inscribed, as o'er the gate of hell,                        135
'All hope abandon ye who enter here;'
None frowned, none trembled, none with eager fear
Gazed on another's eye of cold command,
Until the subject of a tyrant's will
Became, worse fate, the abject of his own,                          140
Which spurred him, like an outspent horse, to death.
None wrought his lips in truth-entangling lines
Which smiled the lie his tongue disdained to speak;
None, with firm sneer, trod out in his own heart
The sparks of love and hope till there remained                     145
Those bitter ashes, a soul self-consumed,
And the wretch crept a vampire among men,
Infecting all with his own hideous ill;
None talked that common, false, cold, hollow talk
Which makes the heart deny the "yes" it breathes,                   150
Yet question that unmeant hypocrisy
With such a self-mistrust as has no name.

And women, too, frank, beautiful, and kind
As the free heaven which rains fresh light and dew
On the wide earth, past; gentle radiant forms,           155
From custom's evil taint exempt and pure;
Speaking the wisdom once they could not think,
Looking emotions once they feared to feel,
And changed to all which once they dared not be,
Yet being now, made earth like heaven; nor pride,       160
Nor jealousy, nor envy, nor ill shame,
The bitterest of those drops of treasured gall,
Spoiled the sweet taste of the nepenthe, love.

Thrones, altars, judgement-seats, and prisons; wherein,
And beside which, by wretched men were borne        165
Sceptres, tiaras, swords, and chains, and tomes
Of reasoned wrong, glozed on by ignorance,
Were like those monstrous and barbaric shapes,
The ghosts of a no-more-remembered fame,
Which, from their unworn obelisks, look forth         170
In triumph o'er the palaces and tombs
Of those who were their conquerors: mouldering round,
These imaged to the pride of kings and priests
A dark yet mighty faith, a power as wide
As is the world it wasted, and are now              175
But an astonishment; even so the tools
And emblems of its last captivity,
Amid the dwellings of the peopled earth,
Stand, not o'erthrown, but unregarded now.
And those foul shapes, abhorred by god and man—    180
Which, under many a name and many a form
Strange, savage, ghastly, dark and execrable,
Were Jupiter, the tyrant of the world;
And which the nations, panic-stricken, served
With blood, and hearts broken by long hope, and love   185
Dragged to his altars soiled and garlandless,
And slain among men's unreclaiming tears,
Flattering the thing they feared, which fear was hate—
Frown, mouldering fast, o'er their abandoned shrines:
The painted veil, by those who were, called life,       190
Which mimicked, as with colours idly spread,
All men believed and hoped, is torn aside;
The loathsome mask has fallen, the man remains

Sceptreless, free, uncircumscribed, but man
Equal, unclassed, tribeless, and nationless,                195
Exempt from awe, worship, degree, the king
Over himself; just, gentle, wise; but man
Passionless?—no, yet free from guilt or pain,
Which were, for his will made or suffered them,
Nor yet exempt, though ruling them like slaves,            200
From chance, and death, and mutability,
The clogs of that which else might oversoar
The loftiest star of unascended heaven,
Pinnacled dim in the intense inane.


# ACT 4.


## SCENE 4.1: A PART OF THE FOREST NEAR THE CAVE OF PROMETHEUS. PANTHEA AND IONE ARE SLEEPING: THEY AWAKEN GRADUALLY DURING THE FIRST SONG.


VOICE OF UNSEEN SPIRITS:
The pale stars are gone!
For the sun, their swift shepherd,
To their folds them compelling,
In the depths of the dawn,
Hastes, in meteor-eclipsing array, and they flee             5
Beyond his blue dwelling,
As fawns flee the leopard.
But where are ye?


[A TRAIN OF DARK FORMS AND SHADOWS PASSES BY CONFUSEDLY, SINGING.]


Here, oh, here:
We bear the bier                                            10
Of the father of many a cancelled year!
Spectres we
Of the dead Hours be,
We bear Time to his tomb in eternity.


Strew, oh, strew                                            15
Hair, not yew!
Wet the dusty pall with tears, not dew!

Be the faded flowers
Of Death's bare bowers
Spread on the corpse of the King of Hours!                    20

Haste, oh, haste!
As shades are chased,
Trembling, by day, from heaven's blue waste.
We melt away,
Like dissolving spray,                    25
From the children of a diviner day,
With the lullaby
Of winds that die
On the bosom of their own harmony!

IONE:
What dark forms were they?                    30

PANTHEA:
The past Hours weak and gray,
With the spoil which their toil
Raked together
From the conquest but One could foil.

IONE:
Have they passed?

PANTHEA:
They have passed;                    35
They outspeeded the blast,
While 'tis said, they are fled:

IONE:
Whither, oh, whither?

PANTHEA:
To the dark, to the past, to the dead.

VOICE OF UNSEEN SPIRITS:
Bright clouds float in heaven,                    40
Dew-stars gleam on earth,
Waves assemble on ocean,
They are gathered and driven

By the storm of delight, by the panic of glee!
They shake with emotion,                                    45
They dance in their mirth.
But where are ye?

The pine boughs are singing
Old songs with new gladness,
The billows and fountains                                   50
Fresh music are flinging,
Like the notes of a spirit from land and from sea;
The storms mock the mountains
With the thunder of gladness.
But where are ye?                                           55

IONE:
What charioteers are these?

PANTHEA:
Where are their chariots?

SEMICHORUS OF HOURS:
The voice of the Spirits of Air and of Earth
Has drawn back the figured curtain of sleep
Which covered our being and darkened our birth
In the deep.

A VOICE:
In the deep?

SEMICHORUS 2:
Oh, below the deep.                                         60

SEMICHORUS 1:
An hundred ages we had been kept
Cradled in visions of hate and care,
And each one who waked as his brother slept,
Found the truth—

SEMICHORUS 2:
Worse than his visions were!

SEMICHORUS 1:
We have heard the lute of Hope in sleep;                    65
We have known the voice of Love in dreams;
We have felt the wand of Power, and leap—

SEMICHORUS 2:
As the billows leap in the morning beams!

CHORUS:
Weave the dance on the floor of the breeze,
Pierce with song heaven's silent light,                     70
Enchant the day that too swiftly flees,
To check its flight ere the cave of Night.

Once the hungry Hours were hounds
Which chased the day like a bleeding deer,
And it limped and stumbled with many wounds                 75
Through the nightly dells of the desert year.

But now, oh weave the mystic measure
Of music, and dance, and shapes of light,
Let the Hours, and the spirits of might and pleasure,
Like the clouds and sunbeams, unite—

A VOICE:
Unite!                                                      80

PANTHEA:
See, where the Spirits of the human mind
Wrapped in sweet sounds, as in bright veils, approach.

CHORUS OF SPIRITS:
We join the throng
Of the dance and the song,
By the whirlwind of gladness borne along;                   85
As the flying-fish leap
From the Indian deep,
And mix with the sea-birds, half-asleep.

CHORUS OF HOURS:
Whence come ye, so wild and so fleet,
For sandals of lightning are on your feet,                  90

And your wings are soft and swift as thought,
And your eyes are as love which is veiled not?

CHORUS OF SPIRITS:
We come from the mind
Of human kind
Which was late so dusk, and obscene, and blind,                95
Now 'tis an ocean
Of clear emotion,
A heaven of serene and mighty motion.

From that deep abyss
Of wonder and bliss,                                           100
Whose caverns are crystal palaces;
From those skiey towers
Where Thought's crowned powers
Sit watching your dance, ye happy Hours!

From the dim recesses                                         105
Of woven caresses,
Where lovers catch ye by your loose tresses;
From the azure isles,
Where sweet Wisdom smiles,
Delaying your ships with her siren wiles.                     110

From the temples high
Of Man's ear and eye,
Roofed over Sculpture and Poesy;
From the murmurings
Of the unsealed springs                                       115
Where Science bedews her Daedal wings.

Years after years,
Through blood, and tears,
And a thick hell of hatreds, and hopes, and fears;
We waded and flew,                                            120
And the islets were few
Where the bud-blighted flowers of happiness grew.

Our feet now, every palm,
Are sandalled with calm,
And the dew of our wings is a rain of balm;                   125

And, beyond our eyes,
The human love lies
Which makes all it gazes on Paradise.

CHORUS OF SPIRITS AND HOURS:
Then weave the web of the mystic measure;
From the depths of the sky and the ends of the earth,                130
Come, swift Spirits of might and of pleasure,
Fill the dance and the music of mirth,
As the waves of a thousand streams rush by
To an ocean of splendour and harmony!

CHORUS OF SPIRITS:
Our spoil is won,                                                    135
Our task is done,
We are free to dive, or soar, or run;
Beyond and around,
Or within the bound
Which clips the world with darkness round.                           140

We'll pass the eyes
Of the starry skies
Into the hoar deep to colonize;
Death, Chaos, and Night,
From the sound of our flight,                                        145
Shall flee, like mist from a tempest's might.

And Earth, Air, and Light,
And the Spirit of Might,
Which drives round the stars in their fiery flight;
And Love, Thought, and Breath,                                       150
The powers that quell Death,
Wherever we soar shall assemble beneath.

And our singing shall build
In the void's loose field
A world for the Spirit of Wisdom to wield;                           155
We will take our plan
From the new world of man,
And our work shall be called the Promethean.

CHORUS OF HOURS:
Break the dance, and scatter the song;
Let some depart, and some remain;                              160

SEMICHORUS 1:
We, beyond heaven, are driven along:

SEMICHORUS 2:
Us the enchantments of earth retain:

SEMICHORUS 1:
Ceaseless, and rapid, and fierce, and free,
With the Spirits which build a new earth and sea,
And a heaven where yet heaven could never be;                  165

SEMICHORUS 2:
Solemn, and slow, and serene, and bright,
Leading the Day and outspeeding the Night,
With the powers of a world of perfect light;

SEMICHORUS 1:
We whirl, singing loud, round the gathering sphere,
Till the trees, and the beasts, and the clouds appear          170
From its chaos made calm by love, not fear.

SEMICHORUS 2:
We encircle the ocean and mountains of earth,
And the happy forms of its death and birth
Change to the music of our sweet mirth.

CHORUS OF HOURS AND SPIRITS:
Break the dance, and scatter the song;                         175
Let some depart, and some remain,
Wherever we fly we lead along
In leashes, like starbeams, soft yet strong,
The clouds that are heavy with love's sweet rain.

PANTHEA:
Ha! they are gone!

IONE:
Yet feel you no delight                                          180
From the past sweetness?

PANTHEA:
As the bare green hill
When some soft cloud vanishes into rain,
Laughs with a thousand drops of sunny water
To the unpavilioned sky!

IONE:
Even whilst we speak
New notes arise. What is that awful sound?                       185

PANTHEA:
'Tis the deep music of the rolling world
Kindling within the strings of the waved air
Aeolian modulations.

IONE:
Listen too,
How every pause is filled with under-notes,
Clear, silver, icy, keen awakening tones,                        190
Which pierce the sense, and live within the soul,
As the sharp stars pierce winter's crystal air
And gaze upon themselves within the sea.

PANTHEA:
But see where through two openings in the forest
Which hanging branches overcanopy,                              195
And where two runnels of a rivulet,
Between the close moss violet-inwoven,
Have made their path of melody, like sisters
Who part with sighs that they may meet in smiles,
Turning their dear disunion to an isle                          200
Of lovely grief, a wood of sweet sad thoughts;
Two visions of strange radiance float upon
The ocean-like enchantment of strong sound,
Which flows intenser, keener, deeper yet
Under the ground and through the windless air.                  205

IONE:
I see a chariot like that thinnest boat,
In which the Mother of the Months is borne
By ebbing light into her western cave,
When she upsprings from interlunar dreams;
O'er which is curved an orblike canopy                              210
Of gentle darkness, and the hills and woods,
Distinctly seen through that dusk aery veil,
Regard like shapes in an enchanter's glass;
Its wheels are solid clouds, azure and gold,
Such as the genii of the thunderstorm                              215
Pile on the floor of the illumined sea
When the sun rushes under it; they roll
And move and grow as with an inward wind;
Within it sits a winged infant, white
Its countenance, like the whiteness of bright snow,                220
Its plumes are as feathers of sunny frost,
Its limbs gleam white, through the wind-flowing folds
Of its white robe, woof of ethereal pearl.
Its hair is white, the brightness of white light
Scattered in strings; yet its two eyes are heavens                 225
Of liquid darkness, which the Deity
Within seems pouring, as a storm is poured
From jagged clouds, out of their arrowy lashes,
Tempering the cold and radiant air around,
With fire that is not brightness; in its hand                      230
It sways a quivering moonbeam, from whose point
A guiding power directs the chariot's prow
Over its wheeled clouds, which as they roll
Over the grass, and flowers, and waves, wake sounds,
Sweet as a singing rain of silver dew.                             235

PANTHEA:
And from the other opening in the wood
Rushes, with loud and whirlwind harmony,
A sphere, which is as many thousand spheres,
Solid as crystal, yet through all its mass
Flow, as through empty space, music and light:                     240
Ten thousand orbs involving and involved,
Purple and azure, white, and green, and golden,
Sphere within sphere; and every space between
Peopled with unimaginable shapes,

Such as ghosts dream dwell in the lampless deep,                    245
Yet each inter-transpicuous, and they whirl
Over each other with a thousand motions,
Upon a thousand sightless axles spinning,
And with the force of self-destroying swiftness,
Intensely, slowly, solemnly, roll on,                    250
Kindling with mingled sounds, and many tones,
Intelligible words and music wild.
With mighty whirl the multitudinous orb
Grinds the bright brook into an azure mist
Of elemental subtlety, like light;                    255
And the wild odour of the forest flowers,
The music of the living grass and air,
The emerald light of leaf-entangled beams
Round its intense yet self-conflicting speed,
Seem kneaded into one aereal mass                    260
Which drowns the sense. Within the orb itself,
Pillowed upon its alabaster arms,
Like to a child o'erwearied with sweet toil,
On its own folded wings, and wavy hair,
The Spirit of the Earth is laid asleep,                    265
And you can see its little lips are moving,
Amid the changing light of their own smiles,
Like one who talks of what he loves in dream.

IONE:
'Tis only mocking the orb's harmony.

PANTHEA:
And from a star upon its forehead, shoot,                    270
Like swords of azure fire, or golden spears
With tyrant-quelling myrtle overtwined,
Embleming heaven and earth united now,
Vast beams like spokes of some invisible wheel
Which whirl as the orb whirls, swifter than thought,                    275
Filling the abyss with sun-like lightenings,
And perpendicular now, and now transverse,
Pierce the dark soil, and as they pierce and pass,
Make bare the secrets of the earth's deep heart;
Infinite mine of adamant and gold,                    280
Valueless stones, and unimagined gems,
And caverns on crystalline columns poised

With vegetable silver overspread;
Wells of unfathomed fire, and water springs
Whence the great sea, even as a child is fed,                    285
Whose vapours clothe earth's monarch mountain-tops
With kingly, ermine snow. The beams flash on
And make appear the melancholy ruins
Of cancelled cycles; anchors, beaks of ships;
Planks turned to marble; quivers, helms, and spears,             290
And gorgon-headed targes, and the wheels
Of scythed chariots, and the emblazonry
Of trophies, standards, and armorial beasts,
Round which death laughed, sepulchred emblems
Of dead destruction, ruin within ruin!                           295
The wrecks beside of many a city vast,
Whose population which the earth grew over
Was mortal, but not human; see, they lie,
Their monstrous works, and uncouth skeletons,
Their statues, homes and fanes; prodigious shapes                300
Huddled in gray annihilation, split,
Jammed in the hard, black deep; and over these,
The anatomies of unknown winged things,
And fishes which were isles of living scale,
And serpents, bony chains, twisted around                        305
The iron crags, or within heaps of dust
To which the tortuous strength of their last pangs
Had crushed the iron crags; and over these
The jagged alligator, and the might
Of earth-convulsing behemoth, which once                         310
Were monarch beasts, and on the slimy shores,
And weed-overgrown continents of earth,
Increased and multiplied like summer worms
On an abandoned corpse, till the blue globe
Wrapped deluge round it like a cloak, and they                   315
Yelled, gasped, and were abolished; or some God
Whose throne was in a comet, passed, and cried,
'Be not!' And like my words they were no more.

THE EARTH:
The joy, the triumph, the delight, the madness!
The boundless, overflowing, bursting gladness,                   320
The vaporous exultation not to be confined!
Ha! ha! the animation of delight

Which wraps me, like an atmosphere of light,
And bears me as a cloud is borne by its own wind.

THE MOON:
Brother mine, calm wanderer,                                    325
Happy globe of land and air,
Some Spirit is darted like a beam from thee,
Which penetrates my frozen frame,
And passes with the warmth of flame,
With love, and odour, and deep melody                          330
Through me, through me!

THE EARTH:
Ha! ha! the caverns of my hollow mountains,
My cloven fire-crags, sound-exulting fountains
Laugh with a vast and inextinguishable laughter.
The oceans, and the deserts, and the abysses,                  335
And the deep air's unmeasured wildernesses,
Answer from all their clouds and billows, echoing after.

They cry aloud as I do. Sceptred curse,
Who all our green and azure universe
Threatenedst to muffle round with black destruction, sending   340
A solid cloud to rain hot thunderstones,
And splinter and knead down my children's bones,
All I bring forth, to one void mass battering and blending—

Until each crag-like tower, and storied column,
Palace, and obelisk, and temple solemn,                        345
My imperial mountains crowned with cloud, and snow, and fire,
My sea-like forests, every blade and blossom
Which finds a grave or cradle in my bosom,
Were stamped by thy strong hate into a lifeless mire:

How art thou sunk, withdrawn, covered, drunk up                350
By thirsty nothing, as the brackish cup
Drained by a desert-troop, a little drop for all;
And from beneath, around, within, above,
Filling thy void annihilation, love
Bursts in like light on caves cloven by the thunder-ball.      355

THE MOON:
The snow upon my lifeless mountains
Is loosened into living fountains,
My solid oceans flow, and sing and shine:
A spirit from my heart bursts forth,
It clothes with unexpected birth                              360
My cold bare bosom: Oh! it must be thine
On mine, on mine!

Gazing on thee I feel, I know
Green stalks burst forth, and bright flowers grow,
And living shapes upon my bosom move:                         365
Music is in the sea and air,
Winged clouds soar here and there,
Dark with the rain new buds are dreaming of:
'Tis love, all love!

THE EARTH:
It interpenetrates my granite mass,                           370
Through tangled roots and trodden clay doth pass
Into the utmost leaves and delicatest flowers;
Upon the winds, among the clouds 'tis spread,
It wakes a life in the forgotten dead,
They breathe a spirit up from their obscurest bowers.         375

And like a storm bursting its cloudy prison
With thunder, and with whirlwind, has arisen
Out of the lampless caves of unimagined being:
With earthquake shock and swiftness making shiver
Thought's stagnant chaos, unremoved for ever,                 380
Till hate, and fear, and pain, light-vanquished shadows, fleeing,

Leave Man, who was a many-sided mirror,
Which could distort to many a shape of error,
This true fair world of things, a sea reflecting love;
Which over all his kind, as the sun's heaven                  385
Gliding o'er ocean, smooth, serene, and even,
Darting from starry depths radiance and life, doth move:

Leave Man, even as a leprous child is left,
Who follows a sick beast to some warm cleft
Of rocks, through which the might of healing springs is poured;  390

Then when it wanders home with rosy smile,
Unconscious, and its mother fears awhile
It is a spirit, then, weeps on her child restored.

Man, oh, not men! a chain of linked thought,
Of love and might to be divided not,                              395
Compelling the elements with adamantine stress;
As the sun rules, even with a tyrant's gaze,
The unquiet republic of the maze
Of planets, struggling fierce towards heaven's free wilderness.

Man, one harmonious soul of many a soul,                          400
Whose nature is its own divine control,
Where all things flow to all, as rivers to the sea;
Familiar acts are beautiful through love;
Labour, and pain, and grief, in life's green grove
Sport like tame beasts, none knew how gentle they could be!       405

His will, with all mean passions, bad delights,
And selfish cares, its trembling satellites,
A spirit ill to guide, but mighty to obey,
Is as a tempest-winged ship, whose helm
Love rules, through waves which dare not overwhelm,              410
Forcing life's wildest shores to own its sovereign sway.

All things confess his strength. Through the cold mass
Of marble and of colour his dreams pass;
Bright threads whence mothers weave the robes their children wear;
Language is a perpetual Orphic song,                              415
Which rules with Daedal harmony a throng
Of thoughts and forms, which else senseless and shapeless were.

The lightning is his slave; heaven's utmost deep
Gives up her stars, and like a flock of sheep
They pass before his eye, are numbered, and roll on!            420
The tempest is his steed, he strides the air;
And the abyss shouts from her depth laid bare,
Heaven, hast thou secrets? Man unveils me; I have none.

THE MOON:
The shadow of white death has passed
From my path in heaven at last,                                   425

A clinging shroud of solid frost and sleep;
And through my newly-woven bowers,
Wander happy paramours,
Less mighty, but as mild as those who keep
Thy vales more deep.                                                    430

THE EARTH:
As the dissolving warmth of dawn may fold
A half unfrozen dew-globe, green, and gold,
And crystalline, till it becomes a winged mist,
And wanders up the vault of the blue day,
Outlives the noon, and on the sun's last ray                            435
Hangs o'er the sea, a fleece of fire and amethyst.

THE MOON:
Thou art folded, thou art lying
In the light which is undying
Of thine own joy, and heaven's smile divine;
All suns and constellations shower                                      440
On thee a light, a life, a power
Which doth array thy sphere; thou pourest thine
On mine, on mine!

THE EARTH:
I spin beneath my pyramid of night,
Which points into the heavens dreaming delight,                         445
Murmuring victorious joy in my enchanted sleep;
As a youth lulled in love-dreams faintly sighing,
Under the shadow of his beauty lying,
Which round his rest a watch of light and warmth doth keep.

THE MOON:
As in the soft and sweet eclipse,                                       450
When soul meets soul on lovers' lips,
High hearts are calm, and brightest eyes are dull;
So when thy shadow falls on me,
Then am I mute and still, by thee
Covered; of thy love, Orb most beautiful,                               455
Full, oh, too full!

Thou art speeding round the sun
Brightest world of many a one;

Green and azure sphere which shinest
With a light which is divinest                                     460
Among all the lamps of Heaven
To whom life and light is given;
I, thy crystal paramour
Borne beside thee by a power
Like the polar Paradise,                                           465
Magnet-like of lovers' eyes;
I, a most enamoured maiden
Whose weak brain is overladen
With the pleasure of her love,
Maniac-like around thee move                                       470
Gazing, an insatiate bride,
On thy form from every side
Like a Maenad, round the cup
Which Agave lifted up
In the weird Cadmaean forest.                                      475
Brother, wheresoe'er thou soarest
I must hurry, whirl and follow
Through the heavens wide and hollow,
Sheltered by the warm embrace
Of thy soul from hungry space,                                     480
Drinking from thy sense and sight
Beauty, majesty, and might,
As a lover or a chameleon
Grows like what it looks upon,
As a violet's gentle eye                                           485
Gazes on the azure sky
Until its hue grows like what it beholds,
As a gray and watery mist
Glows like solid amethyst
Athwart the western mountain it enfolds,                           490
When the sunset sleeps
Upon its snow—

THE EARTH:
And the weak day weeps
That it should be so.
Oh, gentle Moon, the voice of thy delight                          495
Falls on me like thy clear and tender light
Soothing the seaman, borne the summer night,
Through isles for ever calm;

Oh, gentle Moon, thy crystal accents pierce
The caverns of my pride's deep universe,                    500
Charming the tiger joy, whose tramplings fierce
Made wounds which need thy balm.

PANTHEA:
I rise as from a bath of sparkling water,
A bath of azure light, among dark rocks,
Out of the stream of sound.

IONE:
Ah me! sweet sister,                                        505
The stream of sound has ebbed away from us,
And you pretend to rise out of its wave,
Because your words fall like the clear, soft dew
Shaken from a bathing wood-nymph's limbs and hair.

PANTHEA:
Peace! peace! a mighty Power, which is as darkness,         510
Is rising out of Earth, and from the sky
Is showered like night, and from within the air
Bursts, like eclipse which had been gathered up
Into the pores of sunlight: the bright visions,
Wherein the singing spirits rode and shone,                515
Gleam like pale meteors through a watery night.

IONE:
There is a sense of words upon mine ear.

PANTHEA:
An universal sound like words: Oh, list!

DEMOGORGON:
Thou, Earth, calm empire of a happy soul,
Sphere of divinest shapes and harmonies,                   520
Beautiful orb! gathering as thou dost roll
The love which paves thy path along the skies:

THE EARTH:
I hear: I am as a drop of dew that dies.

DEMOGORGON:
Thou, Moon, which gazest on the nightly Earth
With wonder, as it gazes upon thee;                                525
Whilst each to men, and beasts, and the swift birth
Of birds, is beauty, love, calm, harmony:

THE MOON:
I hear: I am a leaf shaken by thee!

DEMOGORGON:
Ye Kings of suns and stars, Daemons and Gods,
Ethereal Dominations, who possess                                  530
Elysian, windless, fortunate abodes
Beyond Heaven's constellated wilderness:

A VOICE FROM ABOVE:
Our great Republic hears: we are blest, and bless.

DEMOGORGON:
Ye happy Dead, whom beams of brightest verse
Are clouds to hide, not colours to portray,                        535
Whether your nature is that universe
Which once ye saw and suffered—

A VOICE: FROM BENEATH:
Or as they
Whom we have left, we change and pass away.

DEMOGORGON:
Ye elemental Genii, who have homes
From man's high mind even to the central stone                     540
Of sullen lead; from heaven's star-fretted domes
To the dull weed some sea-worm battens on:

A CONFUSED VOICE:
We hear: thy words waken Oblivion.

DEMOGORGON:
Spirits, whose homes are flesh; ye beasts and birds,
Ye worms and fish; ye living leaves and buds;                      545
Lightning and wind; and ye untameable herds,
Meteors and mists, which throng air's solitudes—

A VOICE:
Thy voice to us is wind among still woods.

DEMOGORGON:
Man, who wert once a despot and a slave;
A dupe and a deceiver; a decay;                                   550
A traveller from the cradle to the grave
Through the dim night of this immortal day:

ALL:
Speak: thy strong words may never pass away.

DEMOGORGON:
This is the day, which down the void abysm
At the Earth-born's spell yawns for Heaven's despotism,           555
And Conquest is dragged captive through the deep:
Love, from its awful throne of patient power
In the wise heart, from the last giddy hour
Of dread endurance, from the slippery, steep,
And narrow verge of crag-like agony, springs                     560
And folds over the world its healing wings.

Gentleness, Virtue, Wisdom, and Endurance,
These are the seals of that most firm assurance
Which bars the pit over Destruction's strength;
And if, with infirm hand, Eternity,                              565
Mother of many acts and hours, should free
The serpent that would clasp her with his length;
These are the spells by which to reassume
An empire o'er the disentangled doom.

To suffer woes which Hope thinks infinite;                       570
To forgive wrongs darker than death or night;
To defy Power, which seems omnipotent;
To love, and bear; to hope till Hope creates
From its own wreck the thing it contemplates;
Neither to change, nor falter, nor repent;                       575
This, like thy glory, Titan, is to be
Good, great and joyous, beautiful and free;
This is alone Life, Joy, Empire, and Victory!

* * *

# NOTE ON *PROMETHEUS UNBOUND*, BY MRS. SHELLEY

On the 12th of March, 1818, Shelley quitted England, never to return. His principal motive was the hope that his health would be improved by a milder climate; he suffered very much during the winter previous to his emigration, and this decided his vacillating purpose. In December, 1817, he had written from Marlow to a friend, saying:

"My health has been materially worse. My feelings at intervals are of a deadly and torpid kind, or awakened to such a state of unnatural and keen excitement that, only to instance the organ of sight, I find the very blades of grass and the boughs of distant trees present themselves to me with microscopic distinctness. Towards evening I sink into a state of lethargy and inanimation, and often remain for hours on the sofa between sleep and waking, a prey to the most painful irritability of thought. Such, with little intermission, is my condition. The hours devoted to study are selected with vigilant caution from among these periods of endurance. It is not for this that I think of travelling to Italy, even if I knew that Italy would relieve me. But I have experienced a decisive pulmonary attack; and although at present it has passed away without any considerable vestige of its existence, yet this symptom sufficiently shows the true nature of my disease to be consumptive. It is to my advantage that this malady is in its nature slow, and, if one is sufficiently alive to its advances, is susceptible of cure from a warm climate. In the event of its assuming any decided shape, IT WOULD BE MY DUTY to go to Italy without delay. It is not mere health, but life, that I should seek, and that not for my own sake—I feel I am capable of trampling on all such weakness; but for the sake of those to whom my life may be a source of happiness, utility, security, and honour, and to some of whom my death might be all that is the reverse."

In almost every respect his journey to Italy was advantageous. He left behind friends to whom he was attached; but cares of a thousand kinds, many springing from his lavish generosity, crowded round him in his native country, and, except the society of one or two friends, he had no compensation. The climate caused him to consume half his existence in helpless suffering. His dearest pleasure, the free enjoyment of the scenes of Nature, was marred by the same circumstance.

He went direct to Italy, avoiding even Paris, and did not make any pause till he arrived at Milan. The first aspect of Italy enchanted Shelley; it seemed a garden of delight placed beneath a clearer and brighter heaven than any he had lived under before. He wrote long descriptive letters during the first year of his residence in Italy, which, as compositions, are the most beautiful in the world, and show how truly he appreciated and studied the wonders of Nature and Art in that divine land.

The poetical spirit within him speedily revived with all the power and with more than all the beauty of his first attempts. He meditated three subjects as the groundwork for lyrical dramas. One was the story of Tasso; of this a slight fragment of a song of Tasso remains. The other was one founded on the Book of Job, which he never abandoned in idea, but of which no trace remains among his papers. The third was the *Prometheus Unbound*. The Greek tragedians were now his most familiar companions in his wanderings, and the sublime majesty of Aeschylus filled him with wonder and delight. The father of Greek tragedy does not possess the pathos of Sophocles, nor the variety and tenderness of Euripides; the interest on which he founds his dramas is often elevated above human vicissitudes into the mighty passions and throes of gods and demi-gods: such fascinated the abstract imagination of Shelley.

We spent a month at Milan, visiting the Lake of Como during that interval. Thence we passed in succession to Pisa, Leghorn, the Baths of Lucca, Venice, Este, Rome, Naples, and back again to Rome, whither we returned early in March, 1819. During all this time Shelley meditated the subject of his drama, and wrote portions of it. Other poems were composed during this interval, and while at the Bagni di Lucca he translated Plato's "Symposium". But, though he diversified his studies, his thoughts centred in the Prometheus. At last, when at Rome, during a bright and beautiful Spring, he gave up his whole time to the composition. The spot selected for his study was, as he mentions in his preface, the mountainous ruins of the Baths of Caracalla. These are little known to the ordinary visitor at Rome. He describes them in a letter, with that poetry and delicacy and truth of description which render his narrated impressions of scenery of unequalled beauty and interest.

At first he completed the drama in three acts. It was not till several months after, when at Florence, that he conceived that a fourth act, a sort of hymn of rejoicing in the fulfilment of the prophecies with regard to Prometheus, ought to be added to complete the composition.

The prominent feature of Shelley's theory of the destiny of the human species was that evil is not inherent in the system of the creation, but an accident that might be expelled. This also forms a portion of Christianity: God made earth and man perfect, till he, by his fall,

"Brought death into the world and all our woe."

Shelley believed that mankind had only to will that there should be no evil, and there would be none. It is not my part in these Notes to notice the arguments that have been urged against this opinion, but to mention the fact that he entertained it, and was indeed attached to it with fervent enthusiasm. That man could be so perfectionized as to be able to expel evil from his own nature, and from the greater part of the creation, was the cardinal point of his system. And the subject he loved best to dwell on was the image of One warring with the Evil Principle, oppressed not only by it, but by all—even the good, who were deluded into considering evil a necessary portion of humanity; a victim full of fortitude and hope and the spirit of triumph emanating from a reliance in the ultimate omnipotence of Good. Such he had depicted in his last poem, when he made Laon the enemy and the victim of tyrants. He now took a more idealized image of the same subject. He followed certain classical authorities in figuring Saturn as the good principle, Jupiter the usurping evil one, and Prometheus as the regenerator, who, unable to bring mankind back to primitive innocence, used knowledge as a weapon to defeat evil, by leading mankind, beyond the state wherein they are sinless through ignorance, to that in which they are virtuous through wisdom. Jupiter punished the temerity of the Titan by chaining him to a rock of Caucasus, and causing a vulture to devour his still-renewed heart. There was a prophecy afloat in heaven portending the fall of Jove, the secret of averting which was known only to Prometheus; and the god offered freedom from torture on condition of its being communicated to him. According to the mythological story, this referred to the offspring of Thetis, who was destined to be greater than his father. Prometheus at last bought pardon for his crime of enriching mankind with his gifts, by revealing the prophecy. Hercules killed the vulture, and set him free; and Thetis was married to Peleus, the father of Achilles.

Shelley adapted the catastrophe of this story to his peculiar views. The son greater than his father, born of the nuptials of Jupiter and Thetis, was to dethrone Evil, and bring back a happier reign than that of Saturn. Prometheus defies the power of his enemy, and endures centuries of torture; till the hour arrives when Jove, blind to the real event, but darkly guessing that some great good to himself will flow, espouses Thetis. At the moment, the Primal Power of the world drives him from his usurped throne, and Strength, in the person of Hercules, liberates Humanity, typified in Prometheus, from the tortures generated by evil done or suffered. Asia, one of the Oceanides, is the wife of Prometheus—she was, according to other mythological interpretations, the same as Venus and Nature. When the benefactor of mankind is liberated, Nature resumes the beauty of her prime, and is united to her husband, the emblem of the human race, in perfect and happy union. In the Fourth Act, the Poet gives further scope to his imagination, and idealizes the forms of creation—such as we know them, instead of such as they appeared to the Greeks. Maternal Earth, the mighty parent, is superseded by the Spirit of the Earth, the guide of our planet through the realms of sky; while his fair and weaker companion and attendant, the Spirit of the Moon, receives bliss from the annihilation of Evil in the superior sphere.

Shelley develops, more particularly in the lyrics of this drama, his abstruse and imaginative theories with regard to the Creation. It requires a mind as subtle and penetrating as his own to understand the mystic meanings scattered throughout the poem. They elude the ordinary reader by their abstraction and delicacy of distinction, but they are far from vague. It was his design to write prose metaphysical essays on the nature of Man, which would have served to explain much of what is obscure in his poetry; a few scattered fragments of observations and remarks alone remain. He considered these philosophical views of Mind and Nature to be instinct with the intensest spirit of poetry.

More popular poets clothe the ideal with familiar and sensible imagery. Shelley loved to idealize the real—to gift the mechanism of the material universe with a soul and a voice, and to bestow such also on the most delicate and abstract emotions and thoughts of the mind. Sophocles was his great master in this species of imagery.

I find in one of his manuscript books some remarks on a line in the *Oedipus Tyrannus*, which show at once the critical subtlety of Shelley's mind, and explain his apprehension of those "minute and remote distinctions of feeling, whether relative to external nature or the living beings which surround us," which he pronounces, in the letter quoted in the note to the "Revolt of Islam", to comprehend all that is sublime in man.

"In the Greek Shakespeare, Sophocles, we find the image,

        Pollas d' odous elthonta phrontidos planois:

a line of almost unfathomable depth of poetry; yet how simple are the images in which it is arrayed!

"Coming to many ways in the wanderings of careful thought."

If the words odous and planois had not been used, the line might have been explained in a metaphorical instead of an absolute sense, as we say "WAYS and means," and "wanderings" for error and confusion. But they meant literally paths or roads, such as we tread with our feet; and wanderings, such as a man makes when he loses himself in a desert, or roams from city to city—as Oedipus, the speaker of this verse, was destined to wander, blind and asking charity. What a picture does this line suggest of the mind as a wilderness of intricate paths, wide as the universe, which is here made its symbol; a world within a world which he who seeks some knowledge with respect to what he ought to do searches throughout, as he would search the external universe for some valued thing which was hidden from him upon its surface."

In reading Shelley's poetry, we often find similar verses, resembling, but not imitating the Greek in this species of imagery; for, though he adopted the style, he gifted it with that originality of form and colouring which sprung from his own genius.

In the *Prometheus Unbound*, Shelley fulfils the promise quoted from a letter in the Note on the "Revolt of Islam". (While correcting the proof-sheets of that poem, it struck me that the poet had indulged in an exaggerated view of the evils of restored despotism; which, however injurious and degrading, were less openly sanguinary than the triumph of anarchy, such as it appeared in France at the close of the last century. But at this time a book, "Scenes of Spanish Life", translated by Lieutenant Crawford from the German of Dr. Huber, of Rostock, fell into my hands. The account of the triumph of the priests and the serviles, after the French invasion of Spain in 1823, bears a strong and frightful resemblance to some of the descriptions of the massacre of the patriots in the "Revolt of Islam".) The tone of the composition is calmer and more majestic, the poetry more perfect as a whole, and the imagination displayed at once more pleasingly beautiful and more varied and daring. The description of the Hours, as they are seen in the cave of Demogorgon, is an instance of this—it fills the mind as the most charming picture—we long to see an artist at work to bring to our view the

"cars drawn by rainbow-winged steeds
Which trample the dim winds: in each there stands
A wild-eyed charioteer urging their flight.
Some look behind, as fiends pursued them there,
And yet I see no shapes but the keen stars:
Others, with burning eyes, lean forth, and drink
With eager lips the wind of their own speed,
As if the thing they loved fled on before,
And now, even now, they clasped it. Their bright locks
Stream like a comet's flashing hair: they all
Sweep onward."

Through the whole poem there reigns a sort of calm and holy spirit of love; it soothes the tortured, and is hope to the expectant, till the prophecy is fulfilled, and Love, untainted by any evil, becomes the law of the world.

England had been rendered a painful residence to Shelley, as much by the sort of persecution with which in those days all men of liberal opinions were visited, and by the injustice he had lately endured in the Court of Chancery, as by the symptoms of disease which made him regard a visit to Italy as necessary to prolong his life. An exile, and strongly impressed with the feeling that the majority of his countrymen regarded him with sentiments of aversion such as his own heart could experience towards none, he sheltered himself from such disgusting and painful thoughts in the calm retreats of poetry, and built up a world of his own—with the more pleasure, since he hoped to induce some one or two to believe that the earth might become such, did mankind themselves consent. The charm of the Roman climate helped to clothe his thoughts in greater beauty than they had ever worn before. And, as he wandered among the ruins made one with Nature in their decay, or gazed on the Praxitelean shapes that throng the Vatican, the Capitol, and the palaces of Rome, his soul imbibed forms of loveliness which became a portion of itself. There are many passages in the *Prometheus* which show the intense delight he received from such studies, and give back the impression with a beauty of poetical description peculiarly his own. He felt this, as a poet must feel when he satisfies himself by the result of his labours; and he wrote from Rome, "My *Prometheus Unbound* is just finished, and in a month or two I shall send it. It is a drama, with characters and mechanism of a kind yet unattempted; and I think the execution is better than any of my former attempts."

—MARY SHELLEY

# MORE BOOKS FROM BLACK BOX PRESS

---◆---

## Lord Byron: Six Plays
*by GEORGE GORDON BYRON*

## Three Plays of the Absurd
*by WALTER WYKES*

## He Who Gets Slapped and Other Plays
*by LEONID ANDREYEV*

## Royalty-Free One-Act Plays
*by J. CRABB*

## Ten 10-Minute Plays
*by WALTER WYKES*

CPSIA information can be obtained at www.ICGtesting.com
Printed in the USA
BVOW02s2007170216

437032BV00002B/116/P